I0785121

TALISMAN

SUBTERFUGE

AARON RYAN

Award-winning author of the bestselling post-apocalyptic alien invasion 6-book saga *Dissonance*, the bestselling Christian dystopian fiction saga *The End,* the sci-fi thrillers *Forecast, The Slide* and *The Phoenix Experiment*, and many more.

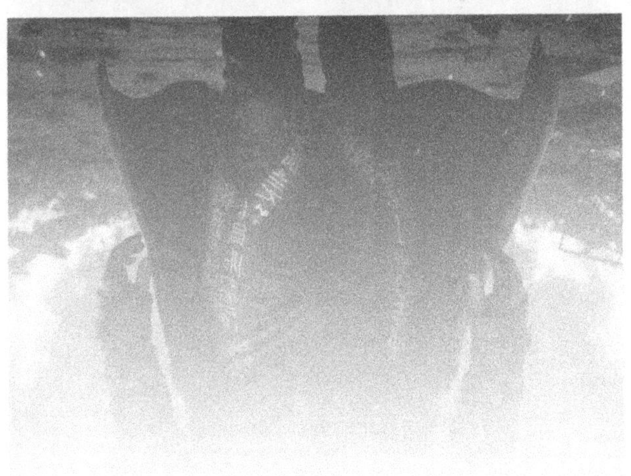

Published in 2025, Edition 1.

eBook ISBN # 9781965372470 · Paperback ISBN # 9781965372487
Hardcover ISBN # 9781965372494

Edited by CM LLC. Published independently.

Cover & interior art by Aaron Ryan & CM LLC.

This is a work of fiction. Any similarities to persons living or dead, or actual events is purely coincidental.

For Sweeps, Bren & AJ:
my true loves.

You have been, you are, and you ever more shall be my
Talismans. I cherish you.

CHAPTERS

"MOST MEN LEAD LIVES OF QUIET DESPERATION AND GO TO THE GRAVE WITH THE SONG STILL IN THEM."

- HENRY DAVID THOREAU

"THE ONLY REAL MISTAKE IS THE ONE FROM WHICH WE LEARN NOTHING."

- HENRY FORD

"BALANCE IS NOT SOMETHING YOU FIND; IT'S SOMETHING YOU CREATE."

- JANA KINGSFORD

"THERE IS NOTHING MORE BEAUTIFUL THAN BEING DESPERATE. AND THERE IS NOTHING MORE RISKY THAN PRETENDING NOT TO CARE."

- RACHEL C. LEWIS

Note on AI

We live in an age of AI. Every day, more and more services spring up promising revolutionary and innovative results using artificial intelligence. The authoring industry is not immune to this.

I want every one of my readers to know that not once did I employ, nor will I *ever* employ, the use of AI to sculpt any part of any of my stories. Those who know me know that I am staunchly and adamantly opposed to such cheats.

I'm very proud to be a verified human. The ability to create is a gift that I was endowed by my Creator, and I will never forfeit that nor set it aside to propagate something synthetic and imitative.

Everything you've read by me in this novel, and in my other works, is 100% entirely created by me, the genuine article. I'm a verified human, and always will be.

To my fellow authors, I urge you to preserve the sacred gift of human creation and never stoop to such lows. Always cherish this gift you've been given. If you encounter writer's block, take a break. Don't cop out. Don't take the road more traveled by. Don't cheat. Toe the line for all of us, and keep creation – *true* unadulterated creation – alive.

Long live humanity.

Also, if you're an author – or even a budding one – I'd love to personally extend an invite to you to join me in two unique groups on Facebook: the *Authors & Writers ONLY* group of which I am the admin, and my own personal group, the *Author Aaron Ryan Group.* The first group is one where you can connect with thousands of other authors across the globe, ask questions, learn and grow as a writer, and network. Grapes grow best in bunches, after all.

And the second is my own personal group. I find much higher engagement in my *group* than with my Facebook *page*. I also welcome other authors to join me there for free giveaways, news, and also to learn why I self-publish, what benefits there are in being a writer-entrepreneur, and more. As a fellow author, I'm always here to help you in any way I can.

God bless you as you use the gift of creation to sculpt your stories. May they, and you, be utterly successful.

Sincerely,

Aaron Ryan,
Verified Human

NOTE ON FAITH

I am a Christian author. What does that mean exactly? It means I worship Jesus, and I serve my God in Heaven. That implies certain standards should be upheld, and that my life should be lived in certain ways, with certain morals, by certain convictions, and with a sense of honoring God in all I do and in all I write. I seek to tell **true** and inspiring stories.

One thing I've always strived for is verisimilitude. I've wanted my books to be on par with what we read out there in the world: to be adventurous escapism, to provide a gritty sense of reality, and to provide a real glimpse into the ebbs and flows of the struggles that humanity faces. That means that life isn't always glimpsed through rose-colored stained-glass windows. It means that with the good comes the gory. With the sheer valor comes the shock value. With the awe comes the awful. Does that then mean that I will ever drop an F-Bomb or take my Lord's name in vain in my works? **<u>Never</u>**. But does it mean that I will bury my head in the sand and pretend that we humans down here don't talk a certain way, walk a certain way, act a certain way? **<u>Never</u>**.

I want my works to reflect the real, genuine authentic struggles that humans face, and as such I want the real, genuine, authentic reactions that come with being human. If an alien is going to eat you, you might not say "Oh, shucks." You might say something, hmm, *a bit more colorful*. But I want my readers to know that I've always struggled with this, and do not mean to offend anyone with material some might find objectionable. I'm a Christian, but I'm also an artist, and artists seek to stretch themselves and strive for truth and reality in their works. That does **<u>not</u>** mean that I need to go overboard and pepper you with revolting material or words that Christians have no business engaging or indulging in. As such, I want all of my faith-based readers to know that I am highly conscious of what I put out there into the world, and am constantly checking it against my spirit before I do so.

Nothing you'll read in my novels is much different from what we experience on this ball in space, and I trust you'll see that I've walked a fine line here, and I ask for your forgiveness if I've offended you in any way. I pray this work of mine provides you with an awesome and incredible odyssey of escapism and adventure. I pray you are moved at times by the Holy Spirit as you read. I pray that you understand God better, and that you know that God knows my heart, and I tried my best to tell a **real** story, understanding that we're all down here, **all** of us, just trying to do our very best in creating what we feel led to create.

I thank you **so** much for reading my novel.

In Jesus' Name,

Aaron Ryan

BACKSTORY

From the Dissonance alien invasion hexalogy
by Aaron Ryan:

In order to better understand the characters and story of *The Talisman,* it is highly recommended that you read the bestselling and award-winning *Dissonance* alien invasion saga by Aaron Ryan.

A short synopsis follows from that series.

In June 2026, aliens invade our world, effectively annihilating 85% of the entire population. They are everywhere, numbering in the hundreds of thousands, hovering at a geostationary orbit over the earth fifty feet above the ground for ninety days. This ominous threat is planetary. No nation is immune from the threat.

No one knows why they are here… what they want… or why they won't just go away.

At first, we thought they were angelic messengers.

We were wrong.

On September 3rd, 2026, they collectively activate, hunting down mankind. Within three months, nearly the whole of humanity – along with all organic life – is exterminated.

The aliens are dubbed *gorgons*, as they possess the unique ability to telepathically paralyze their prey, allowing the gorgons to eat at their leisure. Whole swaths of organic life are defenseless and killed off. The gorgons are no respecters of persons or creatures, and kill indiscriminately for food. Society goes into hiding, and the scant survivors who remain are forced to eke out an existence in the shadows.

In the wake of the gorgon attacks, the military is the surviving remnant. Those with guns and artillery are the ones who survive. Fortified underground bunkers called Blockades house both military and civilian life.

A resistance rises up in the wake of the invasion, trained to fight back against the gorgons and develop the means to destroy them, which includes technology that the gorgons actually brought with them. Harnessing this technology, the military develops 'DTF' weapons, short for Dissonant Tidal Floods. These new weapons employ the gorgon technology through amplified soundwaves, coupled with EMP and explosive properties to expand their reach, which ultimately prove lethal to the gorgons.

The *Dissonance* saga centers around the main protagonist, Cameron 'Jet' Shipley, and the impact on his family in the wake of the invasion. Jet and his brother Wyatt 'Rutty' Shipley are stationed at an underground military Blockade in Clarksville, Tennessee.

On December 4th, 2042, Rutty is violently killed in battle on a recon patrol at Austin Peay University. It is there that Jet meets Liam Fox ('Foxy') Mayfield, who becomes a surrogate brother to Jet. He is the same age as Rutty. Unbeknownst to either of them, as they were too young during the gorgon invasion to register it, Liam also grew up in Jet's hometown of Blue Spring, Kentucky. He had been trapped in Harvill Hall at Austin Peay University since the gorgons attacked in September 2026.

Following Rutty's untimely death, Foxy ultimately enlists in the armed forces with Jet, returning to Jet's blockade, DN436 in Clarksville, Tennessee, becoming a trusted and valiant fighter in his platoon.

During their next assignment at Mammoth Cave with then-Underground Resistance Leader Vance Cardona, they are set upon by a wave of gorgons dispatched by the nefarious President Jean Graham. Foxy nearly loses his life in the deep caverns of Mammoth Cave, but is able to flee to safety when Joe Bassett, a fellow soldier from Alpharetta's Blockade DN282, sacrifices his own life to save Foxy's.

Despite repeated setbacks inflicted upon them by President Graham, the resistance ultimately proves successful in destroying the gorgons in the war of 2042. Graham is removed from power. Foxy becomes a prominent member of the military along with Jet, Captain Miguel Monzon and others, proving himself diehard in battle and delivering one of two Venom-10 bombs that ultimately destroy the gorgon funnel over the Atlantic, which had all along been stealing Earth's precious water resources. Foxy is subsequently promoted to Corporal.

Following the war and deliverance, Foxy marries President Cardona's daughter, Janine, on March 10th 2043. They intend to live a quiet life, settling down in Greene County, Ohio near Wright-Patterson Air Force Base.

However, when a second wave of gorgons return for vengeance in March 2045, Foxy is recalled to service with his pregnant wife, meeting the president in the PEOC bunker under the White House. Janine takes shelter there with her mother and father. Foxy, Jet, Miguel Monzon and others ultimately engage and defeat this second wave of gorgons.

Pursuant to the second gorgon invasion in 2045, Foxy and Janine settle down in Blue Spring, Kentucky, near Jet and his wife Christine and their son Wyatt. It is their estimation that their troubles are behind them. And, for a time, they are. Liam and Janine have two sons, Joseph and Carson, and live in relative peace, often visiting with Jet Shipley and his family. President Vance Cardona, Janine's father, begins the long, arduous work of guiding the United States, and the world, to rebuilding the planet once more.

But fate, it seems, calls upon those natural fighters whose indomitable spirits are not meant to rest.

In rooting out the remaining rogue gorgons lurking throughout the world, Foxy takes his wife Janine – a former soldier in her own right – on a mission with him against the urging of her father, President Vance Cardona.

Janine is ultimately killed on this mission, sowing division between son and father-in-law, and between father and sons. Foxy is emotionally disassembled and outcast, despondent and wallowing in his grief, cut off from his family. Joseph and Carson cannot forgive their father for endangering their mother which ultimately results in her death. Foxy shoulders the blame for her death, and wanders alone in his grief.

However, one day, the medallion appears, and life will never be the same for Liam 'Foxy' Mayfield… who ultimately becomes…

THE

TALISMAN

PART ONE:
THE MISSION CALLS

1 | OPS
June 7th 2062 · The Talisman

Her name was Janine Marie Mayfield, and she was my beloved wife.

What I remember of her is still crystal clear in my mind, though the years increase and the shadows over them lengthen. We had been through many trials together, and no one would dare contest that. I was her husband, and she was my lovely bride to her dying breath.

It was five years ago when she breathed her last.

Some wounds never fully heal.

I will never forget her, though some might accuse me of doing so: some who are consumed by their own pride, who assume the worst of me regardless of my nobility, what I did, what she and I wanted, or how it all played out. They don't understand, and they never will… but it's fine.

We all must do what we must do, and while we do, one simple truth remains:

I'm doing what I must.

I operate better in the murk and dirt.

That's the truth. I guess some guys like it neat and tidy. Not me. It's easier when you can blend into the muck, when they can't lock on to you… when you're able to move stealthily through the grime and the filth and there's no way on earth anyone would want to follow you in there. I can do it cleanly, but I prefer the dark and the mist.

I've never been a 'neat and tidy' kind of guy. I was once described as 'the best natural fighter they've ever seen,' and I think that means that I'm raw and gritty. So be it. However, '*they*' being my father-in-law, who now wants nothing to do with me, and has told everyone as much. I don't care anymore. He doesn't understand. No one does.

Except *them.* And they're the ones I truly wish would go away. But there's nothing I can do about that now.

"One away or one to stay, and balance anew," I whisper silently in the dark to no one in particular. *"Balance* anew. *Balance… anew."* It's a chant, a vow, an oath: one that brings me comfort and resolve in the thick of nerves. After all, it's one more… and one more gets me closer to the goal.

So, I slither here, in this muddy perimeter outside the camp in Chiang Mai, Thailand, waiting for my target, hiding in the cold, sticky mud.

It's been 3 days since the last one. At this pace, it's going to take me three more friggin' years to get her back. I don't have that kind of time… but I've got to. It's been five years already, and I'm up to eight hundred twenty-nine. That's got to account for something. Every day, as I inch closer to my goal, I can almost see her.

As if in response to my cold thoughts, the medallion around my neck flickers faintly and pulses with heat. I glance down. The glyphs on my outfit resonate and pulse once, and then fade. They are a total giveaway in the dark, but, mercifully, they're brief. I know it's just more of the same; they'll explode in color and resonate as I get closer to my goal in satisfying those who entrusted this to me.

One away or one to stay, and balance anew…

I feel the heat of the medallion against my chest, on its heavy but soundless chain. I cup it in my palm and take a deep breath, and as I do so, the glyphs resonate again, pulsing quickly in answer to my thoughts. I know exactly how I got here, but it's still utterly perplexing, no matter how I try to explain it. Amazement resides deep in me: amazement that I should be so chosen; amazement that I should be so cursed.

How I got here doesn't matter. I'm here.

Let's do this.

The rain is relentless. It's like there's a firehose spraying through a colander somewhere up there, and it shows no signs of slowing.

I watch and wait.

There he is. I stiffen, clutching my rifle grip. My scope is on him, and I've got him dead to rights. I hate this part, but I'm used to it by now. I know that beyond the door he just emerged from, there are other sickos just like him. I also know that beyond *them*, there are eleven dejected and anxious women. They're in there against their will, and they have been for a long time now. I clench my jaw, grit my teeth and shake my head as I think of their suffering.

What kind of men would do this to another human being, after all this planet has been through? Is every inclination of our heart only evil all the time? The Bible says that. *She* preached on that a lot. I think of her now, fondly, wondering how she's doing in heaven, free from all of this. *Senora Rosie,* our long-lost matriarch.

I shake my head to clear my thoughts. I can't think of the people in my past right now. I need to focus on my mark, and what happens next.

Without a word, I lock him and squeeze the trigger. A projectile bursts out of my rifle, slicing through the air at

3,100 feet per second. This .338 Lapua is a miracle, and it does the job with all the gentility of a woman scorned.

Hell hath no fury…

The mark's head splits open, and he flies backward. There's a murmur in the hut behind him. Someone else hears it, and they're coming out to investigate.

One down.

The next one bursts out, brandishing a sidearm, eyes wide with alarm and confusion. And another just like him. *Fewt fewt.* They're down before they can even take a breath. Their naked bodies collapse with a thud. I swallow hard.

Three.

Eleven minus three is eight. I'm still in the black, I think to myself.

The last sentry walks up to the hut. He's the ornery chap that skittered away from my last attempt, and he was too fast for me. Whatever he eats for breakfast, it's mixed with Wheaties, because he's as slick and speedy as a mongoose.

Not this time though. I see him flitting from shadow to shadow, bringing his gun up and preparing to spray a hail of death my way. No grenades this time? *Your loss, sucker,* I think to myself. After all, that's how they thought they got me. But they don't know about my suit or my abilities.

I take a deep breath, and my right index finger coolly pulls the trigger as he's lined up neatly in my reticle.

Fewt. This time, he fails to dodge, weave, bob, or duck for cover. His military cap is blown off him. His life is over, and this last sentry falls to the ground, devoid of breath. There are cleaner ways, sure, but, again, I like it dirty.

Eleven minus four is seven. Four dead in exchange for seven saved. My math checks out. *Balance anew*, I think. I give it a minute, watching, listening. The rain continues to pelt down mercilessly.

A diminutive figure slowly, cautiously slides the bamboo door open, gritting on its straw hinges. A tiny Thai woman, her face crinkled in agonized torment giving way to wonder, gazes around. She whips her head this way and that, ultimately taking a singular, tentative step out, and then other heads bob out behind her.

But she pauses, registering something, and her eyes fall to the floor beneath her. She glances down and then looks back in amazement at the ten surviving women behind her. I shudder to think how many are dead in that same hut, and they've had to breathe the noxious fumes of their fellow dead while those sickos had their way.

The first woman stoops to clutch something that her bare foot had briefly touched; the coldness of it causes her to momentarily recoil. She grasps it, lifting it up to her eyes and displaying it for the other women to see. They're all nude, freezing, clutching themselves, but they stare, leaning in, and they know.

They know.

The first woman mutters something that I can't make out through the rain, but then she whirls around and peers out across the expanse separating their camp from where I'm at, roughly six hundred yards away across this rice paddy.

I know she can't see me, but she's staring right at me, and I just stare right back, wrapped in darkness.

She clutches the gold talisman to her nude chest, concealed in her bony, emaciated fist. She smiles out toward me, bowing slightly. She can't see me, but I think she understands as I bow back. The glyphs on my uniform briefly flicker, mirroring her gratitude.

And then they're gone. Fleeing down the rickety steps of their hut, scampering through the mud and streams of water racing down their hill, running through the paddy to waiting freedom.

I watch them, knowing that I just saved eleven. Well, *seven,* to be exact. Seven plus eight hundred twenty-nine equals eight hundred thirty-six.

Only one hundred sixty-four to go, I think to myself. *One away or one to stay, and balance anew.*

I remember the very first day I heard that phrase. It hasn't lost its meaning. It used to settle upon me like a warm blanket; now its insufferable weight compresses my stalwart shoulders, but I feel like Atlas. There's no way to resist it any longer, and believe me, I've tried.

You don't resist this.

You just don't.

One away or one to stay, and balance anew.

I've heard that so many times in my head now, I've lost count. I hear it now as I move like a wind on a breeze, noiselessly, back to a waiting SUV. They'll never catch me. They've never caught me before, and they won't catch me now.

They can't.

There's only one who could possibly catch me, and I know his name. But so far, he hasn't found me. I've been untouchable, and I intend to keep it that way.

Trust no one, they told me, and that's worked out well so far. I didn't need them to tell me that anyway; with all that's happened to me, I am not inclined to trust.

Well, except for Trudeau. He's been a faithful compatriot in times of loneliness. He's about as warm as a fish, but he's good drinking company. I trust him with my life. Right now, he's the only one.

My name is Liam Fox Mayfield, and I am The Talisman.

2 | RUMORS
June 9th 2062 · Onyx Sleater

I have to find him, and Brent knows that.

"You're not listening to me, Brent," I say, defiantly. "He just took out a major camp in Chiang Mai. *Someone* knows who this guy is. And you know I'm not giving up until I find him. This is *my* story."

"Onyx, *please*," Brent grumbles, his beanpole frame beginning to splinter at the midsection, "no one is taking this story away from you. But this guy's a specter! No one wants to read about some desperate vigilante lurking in bushes waiting to take out the bad guys and free a bunch of nude women from the clutches of-"

"Nude women? They were in that camp for seven months, Brent!" I protest, boring holes into him with my eyes. He seems to feel it, stretching his back in protest. Either that or he's just tired and annoyed. I'd settle for annoyed.

"…from the clutches of some Thai warlords," he continues uninterrupted.

Brent Chastain is unusually unassailable today, and I don't know why he is defending my dropping this story so strongly. He's a solid guy, African-American to the core, educated and graduated top of his class at Harvard (once it reopened), survived the invasion, survived the wars of the 40s, lived practically his whole life in a Blockade while I was simply *born* in one. His life has been all about proceeding on an abundance of caution. But that doesn't mean that he's right and I'm wrong. He looks at me disapprovingly over the rim of his glasses.

I frown, and I make sure to let him see it.

"You're getting too riled over this. Too close! Your overinflated sense of justice won't let this thing go. Sooner or later, he's going to slip up, Sleater. He'll be unmasked, and that'll be it. I guarantee it. Heck, odds are he'll probably stumble into some berserker nest looking for somebody to save, and a stray holdout gorg will get him. 'Luck doesn't last for losers,' as they say."

"Who's *they*?" I growl. He shrugs and doesn't answer. "Yeah, well," I continue, "this guy's luck *has* lasted. And he's no loser. No one has seen anything like this since we were liberated, Brent," I grumble, defiantly placing my hands on my hips. "It's not like this is the first time."

"Listen, I get it," he says, standing, and waving his arms to clear the angry fog between us. "It's admirable! Guy's a superhero, or some jock juiced up on a vendetta. It's noble. It's valiant, for sure. He has my respect! But there's no reason to believe that all of these incidents are the *same* guy. How could it be the same guy? It's gotta be a cabal of copycats. Right? Think about it. Dude shows up in Myanmar one day, New York the next, Kathmandu the next, and then Boise later that same day? Come on. These are wannabes, and I can't send you after all of them at the same time."

"It's *not* copycats," I maintain, rolling my eyes. "How do you explain the talismans he leaves behind at each scene? I suppose there's a huge recruiting network and they get a free box of these things when they sign up, shipped to them via Prime?"

He doesn't laugh. I'm not laughing either.

"Look," he presses, "The Times doesn't have the budget to send you out on these wild goose chases anymore. It was interesting, initially. I'll give you that," Brent says. "But I'm your editor, and the buck stops with me, and we have no more bucks for this. Period. I can't continue fronting all of these Nancy Drew exposés you're trying to do."

"Who the heck is Nancy Drew?" I rail. He doesn't answer, and I sense that Brent's mysterious character predates me by at least a few decades. *Whatever.*

My editor rolls his eyes and crosses his arms. He just stares at me, glumly, biting his lip and surveying me as I glare back.

"Look, Onyx, you're my best. You already know that. You've been the number one runner of civilian life post-gorgs. No one can touch you. But this penchant for straying out of your lane is getting costly. So, this is it. I'll cave this one last time, because I respect you, and the people do as well."

A sudden hope rises in me. *Did I just hear him correctly?*

"You have one last chance to find this, this, 'Dark Ghost,' as you call him. *One*," he underscores, holding up a finger to drive it home. "It's Friday. You take the weekend to figure out where you need to be – and when – and you let me know by EOD Saturday.

"You take Sunday and Monday, go to wherever the heck you think he'll be, you lay out your little breadcrumbs and hope he finds them, but that's *it*, Onyx. You read me? He doesn't show up, you're off this beat and back to the beaten path."

"Fine," I say, shrugging my shoulders as if he didn't just buy me a Lamborghini. I try to maintain my standoffishness. "You know I'm grateful to The Post... *and* you."

"Yeah, well it wouldn't kill you to *say* it once in a while," he finishes.

"I just did."

We just stare at each other for a moment. He breaks first. There it is, in the corner of his lips. The faintest trace of a smile.

I win.

"Get outta here, Sleater," he says.

"Fine," I say, whirling around. "Oh," -here I turn back and grin mischievously- "*thank you*, Mr. Editor," I offer sarcastically, with an intentional giggle.

He scowls.

I have to find him now, and I will. *I know it.*

3 | HOME
June 11th 2062 · The Talisman

It wasn't always this way.

Once, I was hailed. I was revered. I was one of those lucky few to just be in the right place at the right time, to have a part to play in it all, and to be able to move the needle on freeing our planet of those damned things.

The gorgons. Such a friggin' nuisance. They laid waste to this planet, killed my parents, killed some of my friends, killed the guy who sacrificed himself for me to save my life.

Killed Janine.

You could say that I never really forgot them, but that wouldn't be the whole truth. They just never really went away. No one 'forgets' something that destroys their whole planet. I certainly haven't. And then, that something went and took that which is most precious to me, leaving me only the fading memories of a life once lived in warmth.

Now it's only cold and dark.

My father-in-law, as powerful as he is, held all the clout in the world, especially since he saved it twice. Even though I helped him – me, Jet, Miguel, Rosie, Admiral Lynch and everyone else – it seems all of that is forgotten now. You get someone's daughter killed, and all that esteem goes right out the window. How was I supposed to know there was one stray gorg down there? How in the heck was I supposed to know?

I don't trust him anymore. I don't trust *anyone*.

I sit here, fingering this .338 gold beauty. One of these suckers does plenty of damage, and I could have gotten one off, sure enough. I was just too late, and then she was gone. Now, I just sit and move it softly between my fingers, sitting here in the dark with my brow furrowed, my right holding a weapon and my left holding a drink. I can't hold her, right? So, I'll hold these instead.

It's 9:27pm, and I'm lying here on the floor wrapped in cold memories. They always come in the dark, and they always come in a flood after a mission, and they're always cold. I don't remember how exactly I got home, but home is anywhere I need it to be anymore since I found the medallion.

Home *was* Blue Spring, Kentucky. At least until 2057. Now it's Olympia, Washington. Call it wanting to get as far as possible away from my father-in-law. From the whole East Coast. From the memories of all of it, good and bad. The odd thing, though, is that Jet's grandparents once lived here. I guess you never truly leave it all behind.

In Blue Spring, Kentucky, after the war, I was 34. By that time, we were fine, and we had rooted out almost all of them. Janine's dad warned me about taking her along on scouring missions. He wanted her and the kids safe. I sluffed it off. After all, even though she was a medic, she was, at heart, a soldier; that's truly why I fell in love with her. Jet thought so too, and though he vocally sided with President Cardona on keeping her safe, he said he wouldn't tell. So, I didn't think anything of it. Jet was my best friend then, and I trusted him.

Until that one got her.

I still don't know how one lasted that long. A rogue, lurking deep down in Mammoth Cave, stealthily surviving on fish and bats, and those unlucky souls who happened to wander down on a fool's errand, unaccompanied by a spotter. I shake my head just thinking about that grimy monster that got her. The pain never really goes away.

She didn't report in. We sent a search party. I was frantic. We found her three days later, frozen, just like they always do to you. Somebody ended up nailing it, cutting it open to see if it was the one. I couldn't be part of that. I didn't want to know then. They found her pendant inside her: the one that I had given her for our 10th anniversary.

The boys are another story. Joseph Brennan and Carson Asher *loved* their daddy. Me. We had a happy home, full of rejoicing and laughter. We lived fairly near Jet, and got to play with his kiddo Wyatt. He and Christine doted on their son.

Our boys loved their son, and they loved their daddy. But they also loved their mama, and when she died, they erred on the side of Grandpa's wrath. They've never forgiven me for losing their mother to a gorg. They were only seventeen and fifteen at the time: young enough for it to hurt, and old enough to do something angry about it.

They were both equals, though two years apart: full of piss and vinegar, and wit enough to match. Though they would never really put in words how much they loved their mama – they took after me in that regard – they each let their love for her manifest in explosive vitriol toward me, the man who got their mama killed. Every single attempt I made to speak to them only ended in heartache and slammed doors. So I stopped trying. Maybe someday that will change, but I doubt it.

My fingers numbly trace the scars dotting my body, freed from that uniform with all its glowing glyphs. I lay here now, running a self-assessment on my naked form.

There's the pink scar on my forehead that still bears silent witness to the war of 2042, when that gorg attacked us in the tank. The faint slice on my arm when that idiot in the church tried to slash me… before Jet gunned him down.

And then, of course, the bullet wound in my other arm when Jet himself accidentally shot me in our final confrontation with the gorgs in DC. I couldn't return to service until December of that year. Fitting, I thought it at the time, as my return marked nearly three years to the day from when I actually enlisted in the first place. Miguel and I shared that bond for a while, 'brothers in bullet wounds,' or *hermanos heridos de bala,* as he put it.

I haven't talked with him either. Not since the President closed ranks around himself.

A cavalcade of memory washes over me, full of grim events and utter despondency that still clings to me with a hungry desperation. These scars tell stories, and the stories aren't over yet. It's all part of one long, continuing, never-ending doldrum of heartache and regret… and nothing a single medallion can ever fix.

I take a swig of this Jim Beam, and I grasp the crumpled note my contact gave me. She wants to meet. She wants to know my story. *Why?* I wonder. *No one* wants to know my story. That's why I'm here, alone: a castaway… *a rogue.* I don't know who she is nor why this is the second time she's initiated contact. There are times where she feels hot on my trail. I can't explain it. I don't want to explain it. Not yet. Not to her.

Not to anyone. No one would understand anyway.

The hot, spicy whiskey courses down my gullet, numbing the palpable frustration, drowning the memories, resetting me for the next mission. After all, there are still eight hundred thirty-six saved out there… but that means that there are still one hundred sixty-four to go.

If only, at the end, I could have my wife, my mom and dad, my sister, Joe Bassett, and everyone else back as well. I think of my mom. I try to conjure up memories of a woman I barely even knew and hardly remember. Anya Rachel Mayfield.

And a dad who was a bit aloof and never got to sow into my life or I into his. Justus Grayson Mayfield.

A sister I dimly recall playing with. Bonnie Jolie. Something about her being equally a towhead…

The biological family that I lost: they're all less clear than the countless confederates I made in the wars against the gorgons. That says something. They're all a misty memory to me now.

But not my wife. I'll take her if it costs everything in me. If that's all that the universe has in store to restore me, I'll take it. That, and perhaps a little more grace from those I once trusted.

I vaguely remember a day when I had faith; when I operated according to a higher calling, and trusted a higher power. That higher calling is gone, and that Higher Power has moved on. It's just me now. Sad? Oh well: grief steels a man, and I'm okay with it.

One away, or one to stay, and balance anew.

I detest that phrase.

I wish I'd never heard it.

I wish those accursed words had never entered my life. But I dismiss that thought as quickly as I think it, because those words are also the impetus to keep me going; the catalyst for this whole crazy affair to try to bring her back.

A thousand-yard stare overtakes me as I wax philosophic here in the dark. What cruel fortune allowed our planet to experience all this mayhem? Did we deserve it? There is no *way* that all of this should have happened.

To see the gorgons annihilate 85% of mankind and lay waste to our planet for sixteen years, and then to come back three years later thirsty for vengeance, slipping past a massive nuclear deterrent and killing off many more of us.

And then we lose Rosie, and it's like Pandora's box is opened and a tsunami of wickedness washes over our precious Earth yet again.

And then I lose my beloved wife.

Then, if all that wickedness wasn't enough, this time, I'm caught up in the middle of it, washed away on a torrent of outlandish duty imposed by cruel cosmic forces perhaps more deadly than the gorgons themselves. Certainly, more untouchable.

Why me? Why did it have to happen to *me*, after I had lost so much already? Where is the logic in any of it? Janine died, and the very next day I'm visited, and those… *things* get deposited into my lap. Those things and this uniform, committing to me this unholy charge and these unnatural abilities. And the voice, always the voice, that cruel, whispered chant, reminding me of my responsibility and my burden.

I never should have listened. I never should have accepted this calling.

But I desperately wanted her back, I remind myself, and right there I remember that that was enough. That it *is* enough.

Jet had once called me his *talisman*. I guess it was fate, but I'll never pretend to understand all of it, nor why it happened. I just do my job, every single day, as numbly as I take the next drink of this whiskey.

But mark my words, whoever's listening out there that put this friggin' medallion in my path. So say I, The Iskander. Mark my words. Mark them well:

It won't always be this way.

4 | SEARCHING

June 11th 2062 · Onyx Sleater

The flight is bumpy and long, and I'm glad it's over.

Brent gives the reluctant OK for me to fly out to Seattle. I can't even pretend to count all the phone calls and emails I sent out yesterday to pick up his trail.

I reach into my pocket and pull out one of the small gold trinkets that were given to me. It's got a curious shape, and I've always been drawn into its glimmer and its defiant mystery. It's got a circular gold top, fanning downward into five distinct gold prongs, elongating and widening at their base, like a serrated arrow tip, poised and threatening. Or a dagger, meant to stab and rend. The orange sunset shines through my window as we taxi to the terminal. The light reflects on it and highlights its edges in its brilliance. I can see my own fingers through the gaps, and wonder what this tiny thing means for my flesh. For humanity.

It came from the Dark Ghost.

This cryptic interloper… this utter enigma.

And then there's the other one. Even weirder. A hexagon flanked by two curving golden arcs, barely connected with the thinnest of wires. At its apex, three triangular inverted spires appear to be launching from the top like some crazy fireworks display. At its base, a stabbing upturned pyramid.

I sigh, lost in thought, thinking back to when I found them. The first time is when I was saved in the alley. The second… when I was brought out of that fire. Both times: *saved.* There's no other explanation other than it was the same guy. Who would leave all these fancy trinkets behind other than someone compelled to send some kind of message? Who has the budget for that? These things are solid gold. No one has money like that following the wars.

He took out that mugger. The guy dropped. I looked up in fright at the sound of his rifle, putting two and two together. I moved toward him to thank him. He disappeared, dropping this tiny glittering thing. It ricocheted musically on the concrete.

Then, soundlessly, like an apparition, he was gone.

Just like a Dark Ghost.

And then the apartment fire. I was almost overcome by the smoke. Next thing I know, this guy heaves me over his shoulder and carries me out the back. Everyone else went out the front. But no; he takes me, quietly, secretively, out the back door, down the ladder, laying me down gently in the alley with all the tenderness of a mother labrador. When I came to, the other trinket was on my chest, dead center, on this woman who should have been dead.

I still have both. I pass them briefly once more through my fingers, and then put them back in my pocket as I clear my lungs, staring out the window at the baggage tugs, belt and cargo loaders, refuelers, catering trucks, and more, scampering around out of the way of this United 757 heavy.

Who is *this guy?* I think once more to myself. Is it even a guy? Did my contact lie? I'll find out soon enough.

It's surreal being aboard an airplane again, traveling the country – being in the air… where *they* once reigned. I was just a baby when it all went down, growing up as a little kid stuffed down deep in a Blockade with my family; sheltering for my life and compelled by an appetite for truth all those years. Blockade life was all I knew.

I spent my whole youth in that Blockade there in DC under General Everett Carson, came out when they gave the all-clear, only to have to return three years later when the gorgs came back in 2045. But the President himself, and so many, fought them off bravely – and they've been gone now for seventeen years, one year longer than they were here for the first time.

I wasn't the only one holding my breath as we passed that sixteen-year marker…

The Washington Post was the first one back online after we killed off the gorgons. They didn't have anybody, nor could they afford to thoroughly screen everyone. I needed work, and they needed workers. By then I was 18: just daring enough to think I knew the whole truth, and just stupid enough to take on a job that would run me ragged as I covered absolutely everything everywhere.

There was a lot to cover. So many had lost everything, and then lost even more. My parents got me to safety in the Blockade, and then joined up. Both are gone now, both from those disgusting creatures. May their planet dry up and may they live under a curse, trapped on their wretched rock in space… forever. I'll be damned if they puncture our clouds again.

I briefly glance into the pocket of the seat back in front of me. They're all equipped with masks now, 'just in case.' Those masks could repel gorgons, they say, and if they ever return, we need to be ready, so now, every plane and mode of public transportation is equipped with them.

But, by the looks of things – and the precious time that has elapsed since – they're not coming back. No omens or signs portending doom from the skies. No. Something new has happened. Something new went down. Those things were flesh and blood predators. This guy's a ghost, and ghosts are from the paranormal.

The one I'm tracking has crazy abilities. He's slippery and shrewd. He can't be tracked. He's an apparition; a specter; a phantom.

A Dark Ghost.

I send my contact, someone who goes by the name of *Cain* – undoubtedly a codename – a quick text to let him know that I'm here, and ask that he relay the message. I'm looking forward to *finally* being able to meet this ghost.

To finally being able to say thank you.

The hunt has been frustrating and lengthy, and I'm hoping it's almost over.

5 | THE TRACKER
JUNE 13TH 2062 · THE ZORANDER

Darkness and light.

Light and darkness.

I hover here, awakening to desire to right the wrongs foisted upon me.

Balance, they say.

But balance never brings me anything.

And now they appear to have roped some new feeble conscript into the fold. Some hapless worm has taken on the mantle of masquerading as a heroic archetype, aligning and dividing consensuses. Stealing meaning away from events as if it were his very privilege or right to do so. Disregarding the very notion of equity and evenhandedness. The scales always tilt, and it's time he found out by my graceless hand.

Confusticate the witless worm. The moronic imbecile, doomed to duty that has its terminus only in sorrow. For a grace withheld is only ever the promised reward: grace unbefitting someone in indentured servitude. I know that all too painfully well by now.

I shall find him, and I shall slay him, and there shall be no balance. These foolish medallions, this accursed obligation and burden that begets only heartache. Some cosmic killjoys out there find it amusing to toy with a soul already laden with trouble, beset by despondency, fraught with pain and desperately craving solace.

I have none for him.

He shall perish miserably in the darkness, and balance with him. There is no universal law that applies to my dealings; no sacred oaths that cover my comings and goings. I am beyond statute. I operate outside of rubrics, regulations and decrees.

My only imperative, and shall be unto my dying breath, is to restore vengeance to its rightful place as the sole, lasting equalizer.

He is known as The Last Iskander. His precious little talismans he leaves behind as sacred testaments to goodwill and to this accursed balancing of scales. Vanity. Charged to him by trickery, and laid upon him by subterfuge and deceit, serving only *their* ends. They once did the same to me, and in the end, no grace nor respite was ever bequeathed to me.

Only heartache.

And so, heartache shall be his just reward. For him and any of his descendants. All of them: cold clamor, unrequited pleas, and a destitute end utterly bereft of hope. Quite fitting for one so willingly enslaved to these miserable overlords.

Tilting the scales in perpetuity that he has sought so feverishly to balance shall be my great pleasure.

And joy shall be *my* just reward.

For I am *his* balance. I am *his* inverse, his parallel, and his polar opposite.

I am on his trail now, and he is near. I am close to his world; I can feel it. I shall find him, and then all shall be restored once again.

For I am The Zorander.

Light and darkness.

Darkness and light.

6 | INQUIRING MINDS
June 12th 2062 · The Talisman

Message received.

1531 hours. *She's here.* The woman. She won't say her name, not that it matters. I already know it, and I've seen her entering and exiting the Washington Post so many times already, unbeknownst to her. Ignorance is bliss. I suppose if she knew how many times I've *actually* saved her, she'd pop.

She's special, that one. She's got a purpose. *One away, or one to stay* – yet again – *and balance anew*, I think, smirking to myself. So what if I save the same one more than once? That really ought to still count for something.

She just looks so much like Janine…

Trudeau says she's clean, and I believe him. There's no reason not to believe Trudeau. He's been faithful. If he says she's clean, she's clean. But I don't know if I trust her yet. I only trust Trudeau. There's never been anyone else he's put me in touch with that hasn't been trustworthy: drivers, drop point contacts, or the occasional operative.

The woman should be landing any minute at SeaTac, and she's been advised that she'll be meeting me near the base of the Space Needle. That's what she requested.

I chuckle to myself as I think of the talisman I left in the bushes where we agreed to meet. She'll find it. She's smart. She'll get the note attached to it, and she'll do as she's told, or we won't meet. Trudeau will be watching her carefully the entire time. She'll surrender her phone to him, ensuring that she can't be tracked, and he'll give her the instructions where to proceed to from there.

Trudeau is a good man. He's the only one who really understands my purpose; my curse. He's kept it safe all this time. He goes by *Cain*, this time, *protecting* his Abel. I'm his Abel, and he has protected me while I've protected others. It has served us both well.

The woman's name is Onyx Ellen Sleater. Last name is quaintly similar to a major thoroughfare nearby me in Olympia. That's a curious coincidence in and of itself, but it's more than that.

Her name. Her *first* name. It's the name of a stone. After all the calamities Earth has been involved in since the early twenties, I'm being tailed by someone with the name of a stone. First it was the amulets belonging to the gorgons. Then it was Captain Stone from Blockade DN436 in Clarksville, defecting to the President and aiding her. He ultimately redeemed himself. But now, here we are again, with all these medallions and talismans. *Stones*, one and all.

I'd give anything for something made of clay. Or wool. Or fur. But here they come again... stones.

I've cased the area, and it's secure. They won't be able to track me. This should be fun.

If I could have requested only one simple thing, it would have been that they had provided me with something a little less roguish and mysterious. My eyes are cast downward, evaluating my uniform here in broad daylight in the bustle of a major metropolitan city. I realize I look a little like something out of a snuff film: this black form-fitting outfit and hooded cloak with the glyphs temporarily blending into whatever alien fabric it is, the countless weapons concealed herein, and the little trinkets I'll leave behind, my short-cropped blonde hair clashing against it all. Whoever the Aeterium Axis are, and whatever strange existence they have in a far-off universe, it's the way they wanted it, and I wasn't allowed to question it.

I remember when I was a towhead, my bushy blonde mane my defining feature…

I feel like a sentinel as I sit here, frozen, monitoring a society that is still gently and cautiously crawling back to life after all those years of gratuitous misfortune. They haven't forgotten, no. Certainly not: but there's a grim edge of cynicism to all of them, and they're all bracing, still, for something calamitous. Their psyches have been besieged, after all. They *expect* the house of cards to fall.

Just like I did. I never fully believed everything was over. And then, just like that… *it wasn't.*

I glance down at my watch again. For some reason, I'm strangely nervous. I admit I don't do well with people anymore. I don't like morning people, and I don't like mornings, and I don't like people. Put me back there in the mud in Chiang Mai, with my cold eyes staring down those Thai targets through a sniper scope and restoring balance once more, and I come alive. *That's* my social ability. I converse through my gun and my fists; I'm to be most understood when my knuckles connect with bone.

But it's backward this time. *I'm* supposed to be the hunter, not her. She continues to tail me, and now she's near my hometown. It was never supposed to be this way. But what harm can a little communing with your rescued victims really do?

I see Trudeau. He's directly opposite me at the base of the Space Needle, leaning against the northeastern supporting column. I take a breath and register the exact temperature of the wind. I know precisely how many steps it will take me to reach my car.

My eyes are drawn upward, tracing the tall steel structure. The elevators don't yet run up to the very top anymore, not since they found that abandoned nest of gorgons there during the cleanup years. But they do go up to the observation deck still, and people are actually visiting it again, desperate for a blessed view long-deprived. To ascend to such heights hitherto owned by gorgons is a precious gift for all who sojourn here.

I could care less, however. I've been higher up than all of them in an F-15 Eagle with Jet, spinning crazily through the clouds and preparing to drop those bombs. These people will never know such monumental thrills in their drab clawing back to the surface. We lived like moles for too long, accustomed to monotony in the dark; you can't snap your fingers and expect society to be suddenly infused with zest and zeal.

A cavalier disregard for all of them suddenly shoots through my nerves, thinking back to the complete lack of honor and gratitude extended to us following the war. Jet felt it too. Oh, it was nice for a while, the pomp and ceremony of it, and people back home slowly became aware that *yes,* that was 'our little Foxy' who took out the queen's nest and fought in some major skirmishes through land, sea and air… but then the applause died equally as fast. Everyone was quick to move on and just forget the whole thing.

And that's exactly our problem. Lack of balance. We go right back to our microwave-delivery-time demands, our graceless ways, our cold indifference, our arms-lengthing.

Quick to forget.

Quick to forget everything we had learned and all that we had been through as a civilization. When that happens, it's just asking for more misfortune.

And that's why the Aeterium Axis came, I guess.

I shake my head vigorously and squint.

That's enough philosophy for now. No point in looking back. At least not for me. This woman wants to look back, I get it. She wants to find out where… and why… and how. I'll throw her a bone and then disappear into the darkness as I've done so many times now, and she'll try to pick up the trail once more, just like any other bone-hungry dog. She'll salivate over the little stories and scattered rumors of some lonesome spirit moving noiselessly, cryptically, through the black of night. But if she doesn't give me what I want, she'll never get near me again. I swear it.

There she is.

Trudeau is meeting her. I watch through these pocket binoculars, concealed here in the shadows of this tree cover on 5th and Broad. He takes her phone. She willingly surrenders it. He tells her to go sit over on the concrete wall and wait. She does so.

Good girl, I think to myself, my lip curling upward into a smile.

She's an obedient one. But she's also smart. Onyx Sleater knows that if she wants to meet with me, it's our way or the highway.

Any minute now. I watch. I wait. Trudeau walks away. We'll meet at the rendezvous point. It's hot outside, and my coat feels like its sizzling, but the outfit keeps me cool underneath. Vapors rise from the ground around me, slithering upward in the heat, warping the view beyond, but I can still make out everything.

Onyx looks around, her hands in her thin pants pockets. She looks east. She looks west. Her eyes stay fixated west. Something catches her attention. The minutest movement registers as her head tilts backward behind her. Sunlight betrays the hiding place, glinting off the minutest portion of an upturned trinket embedded in the soft earth next to her.

Her body curves to greet it. She picks it up, pulling it close. A look of recognition passes over her. She unfurls the note wrapped around its base, and wastes no time, stuffing it into her pocket. Disregarding my wonderful Cain standing across from her with her phone, she complies. There's no trace of any other kind of tracker on her. I'll search her for the rest, and I'm gone if I find it. She knows that full well.

Onyx stands and begins to pace west. She's heading to our rendezvous point at the Blue Water Taco Grill. She'll find the next clue there.

Trudeau says something to her as she walks away, eyeing her. She briefly acknowledges him, continuing on her way. She knows what to do.

The message has been received.

7 | OPTIMISM
JUNE 12TH 2062 · ONYX SLEATER

He told me where to go next.

"Straight to the Blue Water Taco Grill," he said, and then he just gallivanted down the hill.

Cain just stole my phone.

I mean, I get it, but, like, that's my phone, dude. I might in fact need that very soon, especially if this Dark Ghost turns out to be a weirdo.

The tiny talisman runs through my fingers as I walk.

Cain is a muscular man, with a near-Cro-Magnon brow and thick eyebrows. His messy hair tries to be stylish, but it comes off as a cheap hustle. He is attired in a navy blue business suit, no less; obviously designed to throw anyone off the scent that he's potentially in league with some kind of undercover vigilante. But it's June, and it's hot, and his suit looks oddly misplaced.

I didn't see Cain's eyes; they were hidden behind spendy Akoni Sprint-A brushed black palladium sunglasses. That, and his Armani suit tell me one resounding truth: he and this Dark Ghost have money they like to spend. Briefly I wonder to myself if I've gotten tangled up in some post-war mafia, desperate to reclaim power from a world usurped overlong by gorgons.

My negative thoughts and suspicions consume me. I have to clear them and focus. After all, I'm *this* close to finding the Dark Ghost.

No. The ghost *can't* be a weirdo. He saved me. Twice. There's no way he's a weirdo. And I would betray my journalistic integrity were I to get cold feet now and bail. But this is all so cloak-and-dagger, and he doesn't want to be found. Nor would I, if I had seen the world through his eyes.

I wouldn't want anyone to find me, nor would I want to find anyone.

I make my way through the forested path to the west of the Space Needle, hands in my pockets. I gaze slyly around through the corners of my eyes to see if I can detect movement in the shadows. There's nothing. But *who am I kidding?* I think to myself; *you can't find a ghost. The ghost finds you.*

People amble by, slowly, taking in the summer air and trying to appear unconcerned about their welfare, though many of them unconsciously, cautiously, glance toward the sky at intervals. I know what they're looking for.

Relax, people, I think to myself. *We were invaded twice already and we beat them both times. If they come back again, then that's just bad management of our planet and* we're *the bad guys.*

I thread my way north now, and I'm almost to the main drag leading up to the food court. I round a corner and there's a balloon animal guy there who beckons to me. I smile and casually decline. My eyes are drawn toward the food court entrance. There aren't a lot of people around, and I wonder if that's his plan. No witnesses. The hairs on my arms rise in response, and a thrill runs through me.

Not a weirdo, not a weirdo, not a weirdo, I solemnly swear to myself, advocating for him privately.

The food court looms up, and I approach the entrance. Air conditioning rushes to meet me as I pull the door open, and it's at least fifteen degrees cooler inside. A Starbucks greets me on my right, followed by a MOD Pizza. I glance around, slowly, surveying the room. The food court is vast, dotted with tables in the middle, and lined on the perimeter with all kinds of independent food vendors and larger restaurant chains. *Ceres Roasting Company. Wing Dome. Subway. Cool Guy's Fry Bar. Seattle Fudge. Kabab Corner.*

I almost overlook Blue Water Taco Grill as it's hidden on the far left side under an awning, and my eyes were drawn to the far periphery, searching.

There it is. I approach the restaurant, vigilant as heck, warily looking around, caught up in the throes of this ever-evolving A-grade-spy-movie business. I get the distinct sensation that someone is watching me even now.

Of *course* he's watching me. Even now. I take a deep breath to clear my lungs and expel the hot air of anticipation welling within me. He's somewhere around here. I know it. I wish I had my phone so that I could call someone. Call his contact, Cain, whoever he is. Make sure the Dark Ghost is actually here. Or call Brent and let him know where I'm at, tell him that I'm feeling a little like Jonah about to dive into the belly of a potentially creepy whale. Whatever. Something. *Anything.*

Suddenly, I'm aware of an obese man in a 49er's baseball cap eyeing me from the far wall. He borders on *morbidly* obese. He rises and approaches me, and I find my brow furrowing as he does so. This *can't* be him.

He doesn't glance at me again, instead quickening his pace and waving to someone behind me, obviously a friend or partner. *Phew*, I think to myself. Close shave. I didn't think it was him, but *anyone* approaching me right now, under this pretense, makes me nervous.

Fat guy passes me, and as he does so, he stealthily drops a small piece of folded-up paper on my table. It looked accidental. "Oh! You dropped-" I start, and he instantly shushes me under his breath, continuing his brisk pace beyond me. I don't turn.

That was no accident. That note was intended for me. *What an idiot,* I think to myself. This is some elaborate plot to shake whatever tail I might have attracted. Ghost guy clearly doesn't want to be found, and I'm ostensibly dragging potential saboteurs in my wake. I stare down at the note, retrieving it quickly and unfolding it, glancing around me to see who might be watching.

"Help you, miss?" an Hispanic man calls to me from behind the grill counter.

"Oh, hm-mm, thanks anyway. I, uh, had the wrong place," I say, smiling. He smiles back and returns to his duties.

Walk north across the food court. Ladies restroom. Two minutes. Last stall on the right.

My eyebrows crinkle in confusion. Surely he wouldn't be in the ladies room. I mean, the population of the world has been reduced to a fraction of what it was, but it's been nearly two decades. Surely there are more than enough women who still need to pee and would find his presence in the ladies' room just a trifle irritating.

One thing is certain. I'm about to find out.

The last stall is empty. Briefly I muse what it would have been like had there actually been a stray toiletgoer in there, having nothing to do with our clandestine business.

I enter and close the door behind me, straining my ears for any footfalls following me in. Thankfully, the door to the ladies room has an obnoxious creak to it, badly in need of some WD-40. *Hasn't been properly maintained in ages,* I think. For that, I'm glad. I'd hear anyone coming in well before they made it to me over here.

Just as I'm thinking I'm being the perfect spy, I find the next note. This is turning out to be a scavenger hunt. This guy is OCD… or… something. Is he really that much of a threat that he had to go through all this trouble? I feel the tiny medallion he left for me outside the Space Needle, briefly considering whether it's worth it. I remember having our metallurgist test these. There are trace elements in these things that are *not* on the periodic table, I remind myself. This *is* worth it, I remind myself just as strenuously.

Good job so far, the note reads. *Wait here.*

I scoff, rolling my eyes. "Wait here? Good grief. What do I do, pretend to poo-"

A vicious explosion tears through the building outside the restroom. The floor shakes and the ceiling heaves. Emergency lights flicker on, dotting the wall in their frenzy. A klaxon sounds out from somewhere.

Another explosion. Dim, muted screams. I hold my hands to my ears and crinkle my nose, trying to listen. Lots of commotion outside the restroom, but the sounds are diminishing. People are obviously fleeing into the distance.

Suddenly I see them. Two booted feet, standing just outside my toilet stall door, their soiled and ripped tips caked with dirt over blackened soles, deeper than any black I've ever seen. He says nothing. A faint blue light pulses dimly just beyond the door, and I don't know where it's coming from. From him?

I never even heard the ladies room door…

I just sit there, waiting for the inevitable.

I jerk with a start as his voice, laden with a gravelly whisper through muffled lips, utters one thing and one thing only.

"Come with me."

He turns and leaves. Dust sprinkles down from above, and something has filtered into the restroom. The lights are flickering through the smoke. I'm coughing, but I can just make out the lane leading to the restroom door. I try to strain my eyes ahead, but he's not there. I never saw him come, and I never saw him leave. I wonder if he's even still in here.

Suddenly, with horror I wonder if he set off some kind of explosion in order to distract everyone away from us. Is he that calculating and sinister? Their blood would be on his hands! Surely this 'savior' is more noble than that.

I painstakingly make my way out, barely able to see anything. I hear a voice calling to my right.

"This way."

Who is this guy, Batman? Theatricality and cloaked movement. Crazy. My head is spinning as I absentmindedly put my hands in front of me to perhaps block anything I might collide with. I have no idea what I'm going to run into on my way out.

His voice is further away now. "Over here."

I cough through the smoke and dust, fanning particles out of my path. I can just make out a light ahead. There's a glowing rectangle beckoning, and I register that's the food court's north exit. Surely, no one would be able to follow us through this. No one would know where I am. I make my way, half-blind, to the exit, stumbling out into the light.

People are scattering in all directions away from the food court, frantically running: all of them.

Except for one. Up ahead, there's a man in dark clothing, almost form-fitting, with a flowing black trench coat overall. He keeps his hands in his pockets as he briskly paces a hundred feet in front of me, making straight for the International Fountain.

"Hey!" I call.

He briefly turns back to me as he rounds a corner through the trees to the right, and is lost to sight.

I can't lose him! I feverishly try to blow out the rest of the dust and smoke and start to scurry north toward the fountain, plunging headlong through the trees at the southern entrance and frenetically running all the way to the lip of the radius. *I need better shoes,* I whine to myself.

I look around, slowly taking in the people around me. I don't see him. "Dammit!" I grunt, straining to see, my eyes blinking away the detritus still punctuating the air. There's still dust in my eyes and on my face. I desperately search around. He was ahead of me and then went off to my right. I perform a slow three-sixty, scanning all around.

To my utter surprise, there he is. *There he is!* He's sitting on a bench *south* of me. There's a mirrored circular lawn directly south of the International Fountain, and he's on the periphery of it, on a bench, sitting hunched over himself, hooded, his hands clasped. He's not looking at me.

How in the world did he go *left* when I saw him go *right?* Did he double back? This guy *is* weird. I swallow with difficulty, wondering what fate awaits me when I finally sit down with this specter of a man.

Think, Onyx. Believe, I try to convince myself. *Objective journalism. You won't get what you want if you regard him as a freak. Roll with it, baby.*

I take a deep breath and slowly approach him. At length, his head cocks slowly, monitoring my approach. I feel like I'm approaching a jacklit deer – he's going to get up and scamper away at any moment. I instinctively put my hands up in surrender, assuring him I mean him no harm. David Attenborough on some old nature show comically plays through my head as I do so.

Ahh, the rumored vigilante, alone, and secluded, waiting to spring. The best approach is one of stealth, so as not to alarm this truly magnificent creature. Keeping as still as possible and avoiding any appearance of a threat ensures that the vigilante remains stationary and calm, in complete trust.

I'm within five feet of him. He hasn't taken his eyes off me as I've drawn near. My heart quickens. I feel like I'm about to bring a glass down over a butterfly, trapping it for observation.

He's *right here.* He's *right* in front of me.

The Dark Ghost.

And then I see it. Hanging around his neck, partially concealed by his neckline and his, his, *whatever* that uniform is, dotted with strange, nondescript symbols blending almost seamlessly into the fabric. You can't really see them unless you strain. *I strain.* But there it is, glimmering: the same circular gold top fanning down into those five gold prongs, widening at their base, exactly like mine, ending in an arrow tip. It's on a thick necklace solidly bound around his collar.

His voice shakes me out of my surveying him. "Are you alright?" he asks, and there's that low gravel in that voice again. Almost a chant, just above a whisper.

I don't answer him. "Was that your doing back there? You could have killed someone, you know."

A faint smile traces his lips. I must confess he's gorgeous. There's a graying blonde head under that hood, followed up by piercing blue eyes. But I stow my sentiment. Now is not the time to ask him out to pizza this Friday.

"Things are not always as they seem," he shrugs, and he starts looking around, as if scanning for people watching – or searching – for him. He appears tense and desiring to leave. "Did I cause it? No. But did I make use of it? Yes. Subterfuge is underrated."

I just stare at him. This *is* the guy.

"Now, shall we go somewhere a bit more quiet and less public?" he asks. "My car is close by."

"I've come this far. I'd be crazy to give up now, wouldn't I?" I practically scoff.

He nods cryptically, squinting at me under his hood. "You would be crazy. Let's go."

I don't say anything. He stands, facing me squarely. He's tall and rugged, and for the first time, I see his face. Grizzled stubble frames his chin, and there are lines of care throughout his face. When you live like a ghost and run around all secretively as he must, I would expect those lines. He's got a faint scar on his forehead. His brow is furrowed, but there's no trace of animosity to him. I sense no malice, just a lurking sense of mistrust and wariness.

There's no doubt in my mind that this is him. I can't wait to tell Brent. And then I wonder when that will be, since I don't have my cellphone.

"Will your friend be joining us? Cain? He has my phone."

He clenches his lips and briefly shakes his head. "No. Just us. You'll get your phone back soon, I promise." And then he senses the reason behind my questions, I think. "You're in no danger, Ms. Sleater. I assure you," he breathes.

The vigilante remains stationary and calm, in complete trust, says the David Attenborough in my head.

But I don't like that he knows my name and I don't know his. That creeping sense of suspicion rises up in me, welling over into cynicism; even frustration. I work to stow it. *Come on, Onyx. You're worried about your phone??? Let it go. You've got the Dark Ghost now. It's a fair trade.*

And then he offers a meek smile. I know he means it to reassure me, but there's pain behind that smile, as if it's a thin manhole cover over a sewer containing years of sludge he's desperate to keep out of reach. It hits me; it's sad to behold. There's a gravitas there, pocked by years of yearning and hiding.

He pulls something out of his pocket, quickly scans me with it, and it's then that I realize he is looking for any kind of tracking device.

"I gave Cain my phone," I assert.

His eyes meet mine briefly, but he continues scanning me up and down, withholding any response.

"Lose the mace," he says to me, and I roll my eyes and take a deep breath.

"You sure know how to make a girl feel safe," I growl, but I can't suppress a smile as I fish my keys out of my pocket. Neither can he. I slowly remove the mace cannister from the key ring, tossing it aside.

As if in exchange, he approaches me, slowly, retrieving my arm and pulling it toward him, palm up. He silently places something cold and metallic in my palm, closing my fingers around it.

I glance down at it, knowing full well what it is before I even do so.

Another medallion.

He's left one for me each time he's saved me. At least, I found one after the apartment fire and the mugging. From the explosion that just happened, I'm betting my number would have been up there as well, and now I've earned another prize for staying alive.

John Travolta would be proud of me.

The Dark Ghost sizes me up and down for a moment, but that moment feels like an eternity as we reckon with each other, silently.

"Come with me," he finally says again.

I listen to him.

The Dark Ghost tells me where to go next.

8 | FOUND

June 12th 2062 · The Talisman

She has no idea of my intention.

I'm not about to give away the farm. Not yet. I understand why she's here, but she can't know. I can't let the truth get back to my father-in-law… or others. There are people out there far worse than President Vance Cardona.

The Zorander is out there, and he must never be allowed to find me. So, I'll string this one along. As beautiful as she is, she's still a reporter. Reporters report stories. People read stories. The Zorander can read. He'll find me.

And that just can't happen.

So, I'll throw her a bone, hope that will satisfy her, and then cut her loose.

In the meantime, *one away or one to stay, and balance anew.* Onyx Sleater has no idea that I just saved six people in that explosion. And she has no idea that I knew in advance that it was going to happen.

Eight hundred forty-two saved. One hundred fifty-eight to go.

Balance anew.

We're back at my car, parked along Republican Street. I text Trudeau and let him know that I've got Sleater. He'll tail us, pick her up at the drop-off point, return her phone, and then take her wherever she needs to go. I've scanned her, and she's clean. At least, I didn't pick up anything typical except the mace.

"Nice ride," she says to me, surveying my black 2026 Chevy Camaro EV. It's hard to believe that it's 2062, and we're still living with cars from the twenties. They still haven't made any new ones because the automotive industry shut down when the gorgons came, and it hasn't crawled back from the brink just yet. But my ride is beautiful, functional, and, like me, blends in. It also, unfortunately, has the extreme cool factor, which of course makes it stick out like a sore thumb. *Oh well.* "Do all caped crusaders have a thing for black?" she asks.

"Black blends in," I say, steely, abandoning the other half of it as I cavalierly hop into the driver's side. She snickers slightly as she climbs into the passenger side, sweeping her flowing, red hair behind her. I watch her, somberly. "Don't try anything silly," I caution her. "I'm not going to hurt you."

She just watches me back. "Don't hurt me, and I won't try anything silly."

There's an ornery twinkle in her eye, and I decide then that I like her. She's got spunk. She must have been born and grown up in a Blockade, not been forced to evacuate to one. There's a difference. Those who had to leave their old lives behind and compromise have an unflinching grudge about them. But those born in the Blockades, or growing up in them, have a distinct sense of rebelliousness about them: an unfettered optimism and quirky, adventuresome nature. Like they were untainted by the years prior. She stands in stark contrast to those I was judging earlier, ambling by just below the Space Needle.

I turn away from her, start the car, and we're rolling. The Camaro slowly rumbles down Republican Street toward Queen Anne, taking a sharp left.

"You came to find me. You've found me. I know you have questions," I voice. I can feel her turn to me as I stare straight forward, but I pull back my hood. I can at least give her that much. She practically suppresses a gasp as she beholds my cranium for the first time. *Yes, there are scars, lady. Move on.* "I can answer as many as I can, but not all."

She doesn't say anything yet, but I can feel her staring at me, surveying me curiously, sizing me up. Maybe she even recognized me, though I don't suppose I look a bit like I did twenty years ago. Maybe still in the eyes, but that's about it.

I sense her stir. Wordlessly, she retrieves something from her pocket, and they catch the light and glint, drawing my eyes to them.

The mugger. The apartment fire, I think.

"These belong to you," she says, and she hands them to me. I shake my head.

"Not anymore. They're yours."

"I- I guess I wanted to say… *thank you*," she mutters. "I know it was you." I can feel her studying me as we drive.

"You're welcome."

"What are these- these 'talisman' things, these trinkets that you leave behind?" she asks right on the coattails of my words, fingering the one that I just gave her and letting it send shards of light all throughout my car as it dances in the sunlight.

I turn to look at it, and then her, briefly.

"They're *yours*," I repeat. She studies me. "They're a gift, just like your life, Onyx." At hearing her own name, she starts a little bit.

"So you know my name, but I don't know yours. Why is that?" Onyx returns the talismans to her pocket.

I shake my head. "I can't tell you my name just yet. You'll understand why. There are individuals out there who…" -here I trail off, unsure how much truth to reveal in the confines of this black bullet speeding down Queen Anne toward Denny- "cannot know I'm here."

"Fine," she quietly says. "But why the mystery? Why *are* you here?"

"Why are *you* here?" I ask her, sharply, and she flinches as I turn briskly to face her again. "Isn't it enough that someone just wants to do some good?"

She appears gobsmacked for a moment. Her lips move, wordlessly, searching for an answer to a question that she obviously hadn't anticipated. "I- I guess I wanted to know why you saved me. Why you're running around saving people all the time. And, okay, *yes,* I'm a journalist, and it's my job to dig up stories. I want to know who you are and why you're always running around out there like some kind of-"

"Dark Ghost?" I say, cutting her off.

Her mouth falls open a bit, speechless. I smile. Score one for The Iskander.

She turns to face the road with a hard sigh. "You've been spying on me. Haven't you?" she asks. I don't answer. "All this time. I mean, don't get me wrong, I'm grateful for the mugger… for the apartment fire… for you saving me from both. But I must say this is damned peculiar, Mr. Dark Ghost Guy." She shakes her head.

"You don't need to know everything yet." I clear my throat, preparing to spring this on her. This next part may freak her out, but it's worth it, I deem. "You had one last chance to find this, this, 'Dark Ghost,' as you call him. *One*," I say, repeating her editor's remonstration word for word. "You took the weekend to figure out where you needed to be, and when. You laid out your little bread crumbs and hoped I would find it. I showed up. You're still on this beat, and off the beaten path." I slowly turn to find her gawking at me. Her face is a lovely shade of red.

"You bugged my phone! Or my office… or both! Who the heck *are* you?"

"I'm someone who cares about balance, Onyx. I'm sworn to uphold it. That's all. So are you. You care about balance, or you wouldn't be here right now. You wanna know why I do what I do, that'll come in time. For now, you were given one task: find me, and prove I'm real. You've done that. Now you can unclench a bit and take some good news back to Brent Chastain, your editor."

Again, gobsmacked. No response. She's still appalled that I got into their office and was listening in. That's fine. She'll come around in time.

An awkward silence follows, and she relents once more and keeps her eyes glued to the road, which passes swiftly under us as I make a perfect square across Seattle's Queen Anne District, arcing left at the Hyatt onto 6th, preparing to return her to Trudeau at the Needle.

"I didn't mean to scare you. I have my reasons," I say. "You're the first."

"First what?" she answers speedily, yet numbly.

"First to care *and* have a way to get others to do so as well," I say.

"Care about *what*?" she replies curtly.

This evokes a sigh from me. It's all I can give. "About *everything*, Onyx. That's the problem with the world. We went right back to where we all were before the gorgons came. We lost sight of how we came together, and we went right back to a cold, apathetic world. That's imbalance. I'm here to *restore* balance."

She looks over at me now. "You're *human*, right? Please don't pull some crazy crap like you were deposited here as a superhero by some benevolent force dead-set on correcting our ways. I'll jump out right now."

I clench my lip. "That would be painful. I wouldn't try that, Ms. Sleater. You'd probably bounce around a lot and bang up that pretty face as well. Shame.

"Besides, your door doesn't open from the inside."

She scoffs again. Briefly I see her out of the corner of my eye as she examines the door to prove me wrong. She gently nudges it, trying to be inconspicuous.

"Balance, huh?" she finally says. "Okay. Was it restoring balance when you saved me twice?"

"Seven times."

"Seven times what?"

"I've saved you *seven* times."

Awkward pause again.

"From… from what?"

I shrug. "Some of them, you'll never know. You were oblivious to the danger. It happened without you even knowing. You just never found your talisman. But there are things transpiring all around you all the time, and you'll never know how often you've escaped death. That's part of the problem. Gratitude is gone, Onyx. Gratitude for what we've lived through, gratitude for still being alive despite it all."

"And you're here to encourage us all to be shiny happy people holding hands again?"

I smile. "REM made some great hits, didn't they?"

She smirks, rolling her eyes.

"Is that why you keep leaving these shiny trinkets behind? Reminding us to be shiny? Good luck with getting us back to where we all care enough again."

I turn to her.

"You don't believe that. You cover enough stories to see how ambivalent we've all become. Surely you're not as jaded as the people you cover."

"Well I'm not as jaded as-" she starts to say, but she stops short.

"As what? As *me*? I'm not jaded," I say.

"Then what are you?"

"I'm *anything* but jaded, Ms. Sleater," I say. "I'm just doing my part to keep the balance. Jaded is the very opposite of balance. I assure you that's not me."

We make our last left onto Thomas Street. I head for and then pull right into the blocked off employee-only access road off of 5th. "This is where I let you off," I say. "We just passed Cain, though you may not have seen him. He'll be waiting for you down 5th outside the Museum of Pop Culture. He can take you to the airport or get you some cash for a taxi."

We park. I turn to her.

She grunts to herself, and I can tell she's not satisfied. "Just tell me one thing," she presses. "If you're so concerned about balance, then why all the skulking around and vigilantism in the dark? Why the Dark Ghost getup, behavior, all of it? You're running around in the blind of night doing all this, right? Why wouldn't you just reveal yourself, ya know? Make a show of it. State what you want. People see you, they put two and two together and realize that you're the guy who's been bringing justice – or revenge, whichever it is you can never tell – and they'd think twice about criminal behavior. I'd call *that* balance, Batman."

I waste no time.

"You'd certainly have less to write about. You'd call a utopian society bereft of any wrongdoing full of balance?"

She's honestly stumped. "Well, I-"

"There will *always* be wrongdoing, Onyx. Always. There's no way around it. It's human nature. Because of that, I was given a charge to bring balance. That's all I'm trying to do."

She studies me. Maybe I gave away too much with that whole 'given a charge' comment. Clearly that would suggest that I'm doing someone else's bidding. She's bound to look into that. I have to be careful. Loose lips sink ships.

She relents with a sigh. "When will I see you again? *Will* I see you again?"

I gawk at her. She looks *so* much like Janine. I try to stop surveying her fondly before she thinks anything of it. "I'll contact you. For now, this little visit should pacify your editor."

Her turn to shrug. "Sure, whatever. Five hours to Seattle for a five minute meeting and then a five hour trip back. That's money well spent."

"We've met now for sixteen minutes and thirty-seven seconds," I correct her. It's a bit unfair because she's not blessed – or cursed – with the same abilities I have, neither foresight nor insight.

She turns back and stares at me like I'm crazy. I'm prepared for her to complain once more about not knowing who I am, but it's fine. I'll deal with it.

Instead, she silently pulls the handle and prepares to get out. She's forgotten that door doesn't open from the inside. Onyx sheepishly looks back at me and thumbs toward the door, beckoning me to open it. I can't help but smile at the silliness of it.

I depress the lock button on my side, thanking Trudeau for retrofitting my car with this extra security measure.

"I suppose your ride is bulletproof, and it comes complete with grappling hooks, self-drive, and shield?"

I smile. "Perhaps the next model," I say, as she climbs out. "Thank you, Ms. Sleater," I say, and my heart aches briefly. I have to admit to myself in full honesty that it was nice to have a little company.

She turns, crouching just past the door, shaking her head. "Ya know," she says, "you don't make this easy. I flew all this way out here for answers."

"Green," I say. She stops, tilting her head like a confused Labrador. "Green. That's the answer. *Green* is my favorite color. Goodbye, Onyx. I'll be in touch."

She smirks in disapproval, and the last sight I see is her beautiful hips in those tight pants as she stands and almost slams the door shut.

I pull out of there. She grows tinier and tinier, but no less beautiful, as she retreats into the distance. I veer around the corner and pull over, get out, walk around the passenger side of the car and remove the metallic disc that she covertly placed on the door just as she entered it. *And you thought I didn't notice.* I smirk at it briefly before casting it to the ground and crunching it under my boot.

The city lightly bustles around me, and a few other cars make their ways to their random and most probably pointless destinations.

I look around and sigh. Somewhere back there is Onyx Ellen Sleater, returning home to Washington, DC, and now she's seen me. The Dark Ghost. One whom she will eventually come to call The Talisman. The Iskander.

But not yet.

I've seen her too, now: up close, and I'm forever struck. I simply cannot believe how much she looks like Janine. Maintaining close contact with her is not going to be easy, not at all.

But there's something else. I'm so close to my goal. *Balance anew.* I'm close to getting Janine back. Maybe there's a reason why she looks like my beloved. Maybe there's a reason why she's been brought into my life at this very time. Her little stunt with the tracker doesn't make me want to trust her, but there's something else.

Something intangible.

Something curiously magnetic.

Something I can't put my finger on.

I reach down and retrieve the crushed and inoperative tracking disc from the ground, clutching it tightly in my fist.

Across the street, I spy a seagull, gently floating on the breeze, pinion outstretched as it scans the ground below. It trusts the wind to carry it and hold it aloft. Its trust is simple, grounded in the reality that is life and matter. Years of evolution have taught it one simple truth. Keep your wings outstretched, and you'll fly. It's that simple. Just spread your wings, and trust the wind to do the rest.

So the question is, is she the wind, and I'm the seagull? Do I resign myself to finally trust someone again? I can't fault her for wanting to know more about me. I've put her in this untenable position of insatiable curiosity overdrive with my mysterious ways.

I did that to her. I've also saved her seven times now. Was that fair? How could she *not* want to know more about me, who I am and why I do what I do?

All she wants is the truth. Hasn't every journalist since the beginning of time wanted that?

Maybe, just maybe, it's time to trust again.

But she has no idea of my struggle.

9 | SAVED

JUNE 14TH 2062 · ONYX SLEATER

When will I see him again?

His face lingers in my mind. His phrases, recited so callously and devoid of emotion, still echo in my ears, ringing out memorably and hauntingly:

That's the problem with the world. We went right back to where we all were before the gorgons came. We lost sight of how we came together, and we went right back to a cold, apathetic world. That's imbalance. I'm here to restore balance.

There are things transpiring all around you all the time, and you'll never know how often you've escaped death. That's part of the problem. Gratitude is gone, Onyx. Gratitude for what we've lived through, gratitude for still being alive despite it all.

Jaded is the very opposite of balance.

There will always be wrongdoing. There's no way around it. It's human nature. Because of that, I was given a charge to bring balance. That's all I'm trying to do.

All of them, political slogan T-shirt worthy. All of them fodder for bumper sticker promotion.

But that's not who he is. The Dark Ghost wields a sniper rifle, not a flag. He bears glyphs, not mottos. He tosses talismans to rescued victims, not partisan hats and buttons to reveling viewers.

The Dark Ghost is *The Talisman.* I decide to call him that, since he leaves these little trinkets behind. They're a reminder. His very *presence* here is a reminder that we need balance, and that's what he strives to bring, I guess. Or, at least, that's what he's conveying.

I'm frustrated with him, though! I want more. I flew all the way out there for the briefest of meetings, and his scant answers only leave me with more questions; questions that go unanswered and drive me mad. Brent just rolls his eyes. He still allows me to stay on the case, but I practically have to beg him to let me. I decide not to tell him The Talisman is probably listening to us right now. What he doesn't know won't kill him.

I just wish I knew his name. If I knew his name, I get to start unraveling his whole world and diving into his whole story. There is something incredibly familiar about him. Something in his eyes. His eyes are *so* familiar.

The jerk destroyed my tracker though. And I thought I was so sly. He either noticed, or has some technology to detect it. This 'Talisman' guy might actually be too smart for me. I guess that's the way you operate when you don't want to be found. Elliot, our tech guy, said the tracker went dead shortly after I left him. They only got a satellite pattern of us driving a big rectangle in Seattle around the Space Needle, and then it went dead. I sigh again in defeat.

I'll see him again, I know. There's only one question. *When?*

Work is over. I'm on my way home now, numbly driving up K Street to 13th as I head north. The Belvedere Apartments aren't far, and I usually walk, but the rain forces me to choose otherwise today. My hand grips the steering wheel of my old Nissan Altima, still a piece of crap, and my eyes adopt a thousand-yard stare, filled with rumination and yearning. I find myself longing for a jet black Chevy Camaro EV. I wouldn't entirely mind if it was being driven by a gruff, intriguing mystery man, either.

I'm almost to L Street before I even see them, beyond my streaked windshield and the feverish back-and-forth swishing of my wipers.

Gunmen. They're filtering out into the street and shooting at anything and everything, emerging in a frenzy from the Export Import Bank of Korea on the corner of 13th and L next to the firehouse.

My eyes widen in alarm. "Oh, crap," I moan, and then that moan transforms to a yell as bullets fly overhead, shattering my windshield. I dive into the passenger seat. My car actually rocks from the pulverizing onslaught. I cover my ears in a panic, lying on my side across the seats as the laminated glass fragments come raining down. Someone screams. I think it's me.

I can't stay here. If that's a robbery, and all of them have those kinds of machine guns, I'm a sitting duck.

I reach for the passenger side door. Something hot momentarily scorches me around my right hip near my pocket, and I wonder if I've been shot. I press on, pulling the handle and feverishly ripping myself out. More gunfire, exploding around me.

My door is open and I see a man in a business coat cowering behind his car, clutching his briefcase close to his chest, hoping vainly that its dense assembly would stop a high-caliber assault rifle. Our eyes meet, but that's about it. I have to keep going.

There's an explosion of some kind to my north, and I wonder if they've brought RPGs or something. This has got to be some coordinated gang to have that kind of equipment. Otherwise, it's yet another mafioso family that's sprung up in the wake of civilization desperately trying to crawl out from under the shadow of alien occupation.

I don't care who it is, I think, as I clumsily plop down behind my car, whirling and squatting. *I just need to get to safety.* I scan the area quickly, looking for a place to hide. These attackers are brazen. They're here in broad daylight in a pouring rain, *not* under the cover of night. Bullets riddle the cars and buildings around us as they spray gunfire through the droplets.

I scream in raw fear as a getaway van roars right past me and rips my passenger door right off its hinges. Metal thrashes against metal and sparks fly as I shriek. The van screams into the waiting intersection as the villains – whomever they are – scramble aboard.

I've spun to my right to avoid the van, and am incredulous that my car – and myself – are still mostly intact. My eyes, ringed with fear, glance over to Businessman Briefcase Guy, who is about as incredulous as I am. His eyes are suddenly drawn to the sky behind me. I try to peer around my car and see where the assailants are. Rain pounds down around me.

That's when I hear the voice.

"Well, that didn't take long."

It's a gravelly voice, a sullen voice; it's laden with care, and I know exactly who it is.

I whip around.

The Talisman.

He is standing there, seemingly oblivious to the danger. "Do you come with a built-in trauma magnet or something?" he asks, wickedly.

I crinkle my nose and squint through the rain. Is he kidding? He smiles briefly as I'm about to flip him off.

"Wait here."

Yeah, like I'm going anywhere soon, pal.

My jaw drops as his outfit, concealed under his trench coat… all of it… pulsates a faint blue. Those – glyphs – whatever they are, flicker briefly. And before I can say anything, he's gone, and all that remains is the memory of his smile as I stare into the sky. My jaw drops.

Not gone, as if he took a running start and leapt out of sight. Not gone as if someone heaved themselves up a rope.

No.

Gone – as if someone blew out a candle or snapped a magic finger.

Like… *poof!* gone.

My eyes, already ringed with fear, expand until I fear they might rip. Where the heck did he go? *Where the* heck *did he go?!?*

My panicked eyes dart all around me. Once more, I glance back at Businessman Briefcase Guy behind me, and the circumference of his eyes mirror mine.

The rain pours down. A crack of thunder.

I peer out into the intersection. A bank employee charges out at the assailants, firing through the rain. Some whirl and take cover behind the shielding of the van.

One turns to face him. Suddenly, high up, a shot rings out from one of the outthrust patio arms of the APLU building on the corner of 13th and L. The assailant is down. I glance up at the sound; there's only a residual cloud of vapor.

I look back.

A family of four suddenly exit a sedan up ahead, and the same assailant, holding everyone off, turns to send a hail of bullets their way.

The rain dumps on all of us from above, oblivious to the noise and din of humans fighting humans.

Oblivious to the *imbalance* of it all.

A streak of black whisks down from the roof, leaving a contrail of dark mist behind it. The family is gone, carried away on a tide of shade to safety. The assailant's bullets meet nothing except glass and metal.

Out of nowhere, someone attempts to take matters into their own hands, and an SUV careens wildly into the intersection, attempting to ram the getaway van. Someone grew tired of all the fearmongering and violence, and their car now screams into the intersection, heading straight for the assailant. He turns to fire.

Black darkness materializes inside the driver's SUV for only a flicker, and then it's gone – and the driver along with it. And then, just as the SUV is about to pound the assailant into a hammer-smash of blood, caught between hatred and metal, he himself also then disappears. An XM7 falls lifeless to the ground in his place.

The van skids off and blasts down L Street heading east. The rumble of its engine revving up and crashing through roadblocks and cars can be heard as it careens away from us.

A vicious crack of thunder sounds overhead. I squint through the pouring deluge at the shrapnel and testaments to violence littering the intersection.

My car is toast. Businessman Briefcase Guy has fled. I'm alone here in the pouring rain.

The Talisman is gone.

I've been saved… and so have others. But in my next confessional, I'm confessing to being a Trauma Magnet.

Just like he said.

I look down and notice another talisman lying there at my feet.

I've *got* to see him again.

10 | ANSWERS

June 14th 2062 · The Talisman

It's time for a few answers.

Only a *few*, however.

"You forgot this," I say, startling her, as I toss it at her feet. A spasm of fear appears to seize through her at the realization that I'm standing there on her lanai with the doors flung open, waiting for her. But, once she realizes it's me – as frustrated and drenched as she appears to be – she accepts it, exhales noisily, bends down and picks it up, staring at it quietly and not without resentment.

It's her tracker, crushed and dismantled.

"Nice," she says, sneering at me. "Elliot will be *so* pleased." She casually tosses it on her entertainment center with a quick glare at me.

"Sorry about that," is all I can muster. I look her up and down. "Are you hurt?"

I wait outside on the lanai, my back perched against the railing of her apartment, the rain continuing to pelt me.

It took her a while to get home. I watched her as she pushed past the gathering mass of looky-loos and rubberneckers who just always seem to have to get a glimpse and hold up traffic. Eventually, she pulled her Altima over to the curb and abandoned it, walking the rest of the way. Marching angrily through a downpour in high heels while carrying a pesky grudge and craving answers must really be a pain. I wouldn't know. I don't wear high heels.

The truth is that she might have been killed, and she's pissed. She has every right to be. I've been there. Visions of that cave, that horrible cave, when Joe Bassett saved me. The same cave where my beloved bride lost her life. When Joe saved me during the war, I was *that* close to going out forever, when he sacrificed himself for me. To this day, I owe him the debt of my life since he gave his.

One away or one to stay, and balance anew, I think to myself. *Eight hundred forty-nine saved. One hundred fifty-one to go.*

Just before the van sped away, I saved the assailant from becoming a ham-sandwich when that rogue SUV powered into the intersection. He was so frightened and had no idea what had just happened; it was a while before I could get him to open his eyes and *keep* them open.

I slapped him silly and scared the piss out of him when I got him alone in the alleyway. He swore that he'd turn over a new leaf and was only trying to help his older brother in the robbery. I made sure to dole out one more kick as he fled. Last I saw him, he was nursing a sprained ankle and disappeared around a corner in the opposite direction from the getaway van.

And now I'm here.

"What? *No*, I'm not hurt, but shouldn't *you* be? What the heck was that? I want answers, Mr. Mystery Man," she rails, eyes flaring and advancing toward me. She obviously doesn't appreciate that I just suddenly appear on her lanai, and I guess that she is now resenting that I continue to dangle these carrots in front of her.

Stop getting into trouble, and I'll stop having to rescue you, I think to myself.

"You keep showing up in the nick of time to save me, and *yes,* I'm grateful, but for crying out loud, I'm starting to think all of this is staged!" she growls.

I can only scowl at her.

"You think I'm setting up these little circumstances to save just *you.*"

It isn't a question.

She stares at me, her mouth agape. My words may have sounded like an indictment, sure enough. I might be misreading her, but I don't care. She slows her pace, stopping to size me up once more, head to toe.

"Well, yeah! I mean…" -here she pauses, desperately trying to think through the noise in her brain- "I don't know, it sure seems that way!"

I click my tongue and shake my head. "The world is a big place, Onyx. Too big for just one person. Surely you've heard of everywhere *else* I've been… of all the souls saved by now… or you wouldn't have such a need to find me. You forgot about balance."

"*Screw* balance, dude," she says, and she snatches up a blanket draping her couch, advancing toward me once more out here. "And come in, for crying out loud. I don't know who you are or where you're from, but surely you catch colds here and there too?"

"I catch colds," I offer, nonchalantly.

The rain doesn't faze me. She studies me, seeing me out here framed against the darkening sky. I'm sure the occasional flashes of lightning betray my muscular form straining underneath my trench coat. The glyphs on my outfit are dim now. But I don't come in.

She shakes her head. "Fine. Have it your way. At least tell me your real first name. Give me *something* to go on, Talisman."

Oh, so she's calling me Talisman now. I kind of liked 'Dark Ghost.'

I just stare at Onyx. The suspense must be killing her. "My name is ----." A well-timed crack of thunder stabs through the air outside, obscuring my words. I timed it just right. She can see my mouth moving, and I guess she can tell my name starts with an L, but it's clear she misses the rest. She strains her head.

"What?" she asks. "Bad timing, man."

I snort a wicked chuckle. "Liam. My name is Liam, Onyx. Pleased to meet you."

She looks me up and down, a bit sidelong as she's now clearly hoping I'm telling her the truth. There are hundreds of Liams in the world, I'm sure… I have nothing to fear in divulging only my first name. And, frankly, it might be nice to be on a first-name basis with someone other than Trudeau, first name Wayne.

"Fine," she says, playing it cool. "*Sooo* nice to meet you, Mr. Liam Dark Ghost Talisman. Now will you *please* come in out of the rain." This time, she doesn't intend *her* statement as a question.

So, this Talisman strides into her apartment, slowly. My boots squeak on her tile floor underfoot, leaving scattered waffle puddle patterns as I walk in, quietly. There's a subtle cockiness to her as she watches me. She appears drawn to my eyes. They – and, previously, my hair – have always been my best features. Janine sure loved both.

"What do you want here, 'Liam,' is it?" she makes sure to scoff at my name. "If that's really even your name."

"It is, I promise you."

"You promise me." She dismisses me, walking over to the fridge and grabbing a Stroh's bottle, prying the lid off with her teeth and spitting it cavalierly into the recycling bin she's flicked open with her foot. Aerosmith plays lightly in the background.

"Impressive," I compliment.

She plops down onto her easy chair facing the lanai. Thunder cracks outside again. The sound of pelting rain reverberates inside, taunting the two of us with noise as the floor of the lanai dances and twinkles in the splash of the mirrored evening sky.

She takes a deep sip, swallows, and just watches me. Wordlessly, she motions for me to sit on her couch. I eye the couch, and then slowly walk over to sit down, hoping against hope that she has another bottle of that Stroh's. If I'm lucky, we might be singing roadside tavern ditties by the end of the night, the best of friends.

She starts to say something, but I beat her to the punch.

"Yes, I'm human. Yes, I have certain abilities. Yes, it's a blessing *and* a curse. And *no*, I'm not a superhero, Onyx."

Her eyes squint as she stares at me. I can hear her clock ticking. Suddenly, she grunts out an obnoxious burp, following her impressive belch with a nonchalant "Well, that's good to know. But you didn't answer my other question."

"What question was that?"

"Who's your favorite Beatle?"

I can't suppress a slight chuckle through my nose. My eyes fall to the floor, but then they're back up once more, meeting her cynical orbs. I'll keep my answer a mystery… at least for now.

"Why *are* you here, Liam?" she asks matter-of-factly, but there's a definite note of annoyance in the question.

I shrug. "Well, if you prefer it, I can simply leave you alone. I just thought you might like some answers after you flew all the way out to Seattle and back for such a short, answer-less five minute visit."

"*Sixteen* minutes, you said," she corrects me.

I smile.

She grunts. "You just thought I might like some answers, though, huh?"

"I did. I've given it some thought, and perhaps it's only fair and fitting for me to reward you for your pursuit of me. I can do that much. However, it won't be easy – for you *or* for me. And I'm afraid… that I must state some conditions in advance."

"Name them," she says, squinting at me.

"You must never *ever* publish my real name."

"Fine. Next?"

She is one to get right to the point. "You must also never divulge who I was before the Talisman came into being."

"Before *you* came into being, you mean?"

"Correct. Before I became him and accepted this charge."

"What charge? And what happens if I do?"

"We'll cross that bridge when we get there. Just remember what I told you. There is someone out there who cannot know who, nor where, I am. Swear it to me that you will keep me safely anonymous. If you don't, you jeopardize my entire mission."

Another long sip. Her eyes continue to squint at me over her Stroh's. "Alright then. Answer me this. How is it that you know these things are going to happen? Did you know I was going to get mugged? Did you know about the apartment fire, and- and… today?"

I nod. "Yes, I did."

"How? I'm listening."

I start to answer.

"Hold on," she says, instinct kicking in. She reaches over and fetches her phone. As she places it on the coffee table between us, I glance down. She has the voice memo app open and recording. She silently waves me on to continue, quickly gulping down more Stroh's.

This is where you decide to trust, Liam, I say to myself. This, truly, is letting the cat out of the bag, depending on how deep she wants to take it. I take a deep breath.

"I can't explain exactly *how* it's given, Onyx. I can only state that it *was* given."

"When?" she asks, quickly.

A quick vision of Janine, frozen before that creature, flashes through my mind. I shut my eyes briefly to clear it.

"August – 4th, 2057."

"That long ago?"

I nod.

"What happened?"

Another deep breath. *Here goes.*

"I was," -here I stop myself, not wanting to reveal too precise of a location. After all, trust can still have guardrails- "on the road in Kentucky. I was in a state of grief. I had just lost my wife." At that detail, Onyx flinches. It's subtle, but I register it. "I was stumbling along Flint Ridge Road." She wouldn't know where that road is, and I doubt she'll be able to trace it even if she looks it up later. There's a slight reaction from her, but this time of subtle amazement. "I needed… space. I had left everyone behind and needed to just be alone.

"Well, I was stumbling down the road through the forest, consumed by my grief. My wife had just been taken from me. Something… caught my eye."

"Something?"

"Up ahead. To the northeast. A glow. Something was radiating… pulsating… in the forest, just north of the road. I had no idea my life was about to change."

She sits quietly, studying me patiently, but her curiosity pushes the next question out of her. "What did you find? What did you see?"

I gather air into my lungs, slowly, letting it out like a deflating tire. "To this day, I don't really know what it was. But it was… something beautiful. Captivating. Alluring. It – defied the laws of physics. All I can remember is that it was some kind of craft or something. It was spinning in all directions, surrounded by rings orbiting it in a counter spin. Something kept it aloft, all the while humming and pulsating."

"So, a UFO? You saw a freaking UFO? I mean, what color was it? How big was it?"

"Primarily red. But also some blues and auburn tints. It was probably the size of my car or… something. Maybe a little bigger."

She leaned in toward me. "What did it do, Liam?"

I realize just then that I had never told this story to a single soul except Jet. He is the last one from my old life that I had spoken to. I'm lost in thought, carried back on a wave of regret and memory. Jet didn't believe me. He didn't want to. He's had enough. My story smacked too much of otherworldly intrusion into our wounded reality, and he wanted no part of it. He began to shut me out, and that's when I left.

"Liam?" a soft voice pries, and I'm jerked back to Onyx and her living room.

I gather myself. "Sorry. Just… remembering. I was 'drawn' to it, you could say. It was mesmerizing. Gorgeous. Enchanting. Something was calling me in there, and," -here I grimace as I take in the memory of what I had sought to block out- "it… sounded like my wife's voice."

"The one who had died?"

"I've only ever had one."

She nods sympathetically, clenching her lip. Her eyes bore holes into me, slave to the intrigue of my story, held sway by its mystery. "What happened then?" she asks.

"*One away or one to stay, and balance anew,* the voice chanted, over and over and over as I drew near, and I was weeping." I can feel my brows furrow at the misery of it all, resurfacing in my mind. "Weeping uncontrollably. Sobbing at having lost her, sobbing at hearing her voice. Sobbing.

"And that's when the light hit me."

Onyx leans forward with her elbows on her knees, her fingers clasped, her neck craned into me. "What light? What light, Liam?"

It's then that I discover that I'm sweating… *and* slightly trembling. Recounting this story, even to myself, has never been easy. I'd just as soon dismiss it and humbly accept my charge; just go about my business without remembering precisely why.

I steel myself to continue, bringing my eyes up to face hers. "Something… another one of them, I don't know. Another craft must have seized me while the one held me in its gaze. It was almost like a gorgon, but it was… peaceful. No pain. It held me, and then it released me, and I was still alive. I was still me, but – *not* me. I felt different. I- I fell to the ground and then I must have blacked out. The stars wheeled overhead, and I just lay there. I never saw the crafts leave."

Onyx starts to say something, then stops herself.

"When I awoke, it was the next day, and Jet was shaking me."

"Jet?"

Crap, I think to myself. *Think, Liam! You can't give her names! You're losing control!* "Uh, Jetzenburg. My buddy. He- they- he found me lying there. I was – arrayed in this," I say, fanning my arms out and looking down over my chest and torso. Onyx's eyes follow me, studying my outfit. "I don't know where it came from, other than it came from them."

"The beings in the craft you saw," she states.

"Them," I repeat. "I have no idea who they even really are, Onyx. I still don't. All I know is that we made it back to Blue-" -here I pause, fortunately having the presence of mind again to obscure names- "to *home*; I was practically catatonic the whole way. Jet said he couldn't get a word out of me. I was in grief, I was in this outfit all the sudden, everything had changed. And then there were all the talismans. Chests of them, sitting in the bedroom of our home."

I shook my head, trying to pretend confused. I almost slipped again with Blue Spring. "I don't know. I just- I don't know. Everything was a blur. It still is. But when I realized what had happened, I found myself in this getup, and I was suddenly able to see things. Before they happened. I was always a good fighter, but… now I knew where the bad guys would be, and what they would do. Where accidents would happen. Where and when tragedies would occur. I could do some pretty incredible things." I take a deep breath and attempt a humble laugh.

"Like what?"

If there's anything I've learned in a lifetime of combat, it's been show, don't tell. "Well, like this."

The glyphs on my guise flicker to life, glowing a faint cerulean blue. And like a sudden vapor or a ballooning mist, I'm gone, back out on the patio.

Onyx gasps and leans forward, looking around frantically. She finally spots me standing there once more.

"Oh my Go-"

"It's not the first time you've seen that, of course," I say, holding out my hands in defense. "That's precisely what I had to do in the intersection today at the robbery." I begin to stride in once more to her apartment. Once more, the watery waffle deposits from my boots. Once more, the squeak of my rubber soles. I stop, standing behind the couch this time, bending over and resting my palms on it, watching her. "How do you think I got to you so fast?"

She swallows, nervously. "I've- just- never seen anything like that before, man. It's truly remarkable. You certainly are an intriguing creature with many abilities."

I nod. "There are those, however, who would seek to take advantage of it. It's entirely this suit. This medallion. I can't do any of this myself. But there's the other issue I mentioned."

"Which is?" She nervously sits back and lifts her Stroh's bottle to her lips again, taking a swig. Her hands are shaking, and the beer sloshes around inside fitfully in response to her erratic movements.

"Are you ok, Onyx?" I ask.

She waves her hand in the air, dismissing it as she swallows. "I'm fine, man. I'm fine. Just- this is all crazy and- new. I mean, what the heck are you now, right? You get some cosmic suit, you can teleport, you can see the future, you're out there saving people. Just- give me a minute to absorb it all."

"I know it's a lot."

She rolls her eyes and tilts her head as she imbibes more alcohol, swallowing, and grunting, "Understatement." There's a chuckle somewhere in there. She shakes her head. "What's the other issue?"

I stare at her deeply. "It's the reason why you can't mention my name. You're in danger even by reporting this story, because you become a link. A link to me. And there are relations of mine – sundered, admittedly – but who I must protect. You reveal who I am, their lives are in jeopardy. And once more, we have imbalance. You must tell *no one*."

"I don't get it with this whole imbalance thing. Why is that so important to you? What's your stake in all of it?" she asks.

I grit my teeth and take another breath. "Well, this is the part of the story I haven't told you. My wife died by a gorgon, Onyx. These beings, these – whatever they are – promised me that they can bring her back. Life for life. I was given what you might call a quota. A demand."

She squints again. "What demand?"

"One thousand lives."

She frowns. "One thousand lives for what?"

"To bring her back," I say.

"Wait – so you have to save one thousand lives in order for them to bring her back? One thousand lives saved in exchange for just one life returned?"

"She's not just one life. She's my *wife*, Onyx. They offered it to me as I stood there, in *her* voice. It was *her*. She will be returned to me once I've saved one thousand lives. *Balance.* Every time a life is saved by me, I get a little closer to bringing her back. Today's attack puts me at eight hundred forty-nine saved. That's one hundred fifty-one to go, Onyx. I'm almost there."

She pauses, staring at me. Onyx takes a deep breath and slowly rises, leaving her phone on the coffee table between us. She approaches slowly, and there's an air of care about her. She won't meet my eyes as she crosses her arms and stares at the floor. "And what would have happened if you had refused?"

"Fall short, fail, lose the medallion or abandon my obligation," I reply to her, "and the lost love stays dead. Not only that, someone else I care about dies as well. No pressure, right?"

She gawks at me in amazement. "What a taskmaster, this- this- whoever it is. Crappy deal, if you ask me."

"Not if it's for love. Love is powerful, Onyx. It's what we all need – and lost. But there is one bit of solace. I *can* resume my mission, but the lives saved requirement doubles as a penalty for the break. Ergo, I'm bound to complete it, or I'm in it forever. This medallion," -here I tap the heavy gold circle hanging around my neck- "gives me the foresight to know when something awful is going to happen. It also conveys to me unique powers, including the ability to teleport at will. My only weakness seems to be the inherent moral dilemma."

"Which is?" she asks nearly immediately.

"Well," I respond, "aside from whether or not I continue in it, do I choose only the 'big' saves with large numbers? Or doesn't *every* life matter? I know the answer. I've saved so many already. But – there's an awful flip-side to it. A cost. I can take a life as long as it means that I'm saving more lives than I'm taking. I confess I've become numb to the taking of lives as long as balance is achieved. *One away, or one to stay, and balance anew,*" I chant, half-mockingly.

She just stares at me, her eyes boring holes through me. At length, she takes a deep breath.

"Liam, I don't mean to be rude – I mean that, honestly – but is it at all possible you were so steeped in grief that you were maybe… delusional? Please don't be mad, man – I'm just asking. Is there a chance any of this was dreamt up? Hallucinated, even? Possibly?" She finally meets my eyes.

I just stare at her, coldly. "A fair question, Onyx. Is this a delusion?" Where I was resting my palms, there are now only two faint depressions inflating back to their proper shape. My palms are no longer there; they're with me, further back in her apartment, standing in her bedroom doorway. Her eyes dart over to me there.

And then I'm gone once more, leaving only a mist, materializing yet again, this time behind her, at the threshold to her kitchenette. Her head whips toward me in surprise as her breath catches. "Do you call that a hallucination? And what about the talismans they gave me? How much more proof does one reporter need?"

She's almost panting with excitement and alarm.

And that's when my suit flashes. I hear the voice. *One away, and one to stay, and balance anew…*

I listen. The coordinates are given. Latitude 22.228057, Longitude -159.480792. Princeville, Kauai. I see the landslide. It's imminent. The wedding is in full swing. I see the photographer inching nearer, yet asking them to step back a bit more. It's a large group of them. They're all in danger.

"I have to go."

"What?" she asks, shocked. "Why? You can't just-"

"I have to go, Onyx. I'll return."

"Wait-"

I barely hear her plea.

The mist takes me.

One away or one to stay, and balance anew.

There are people to save now.

It'll be time for more questions later.

11 | HUNTING
June 14th 2062 · The Zorander

It is all drudgery, all of it.

Drudgery and monotony, the uttermost end of despair all-consuming, driving one on as with a whip.

That is the fate for all who venture to trust these curs; these otherworldly demon taskmasters with their overinflated sense of scale.

Balance: what a farce.

There *is* no balance except for what I bring. Light, and darkness, darkness and light, I say again.

For the false promise of eventual restoration, one soul dares cross the gulf separating free will from servitude. Bygones of knowing and being known, significance and purpose crumble in their wake, all consumed by this newfound fire.

But fire? It scorches; it consumes. It seizes upon all our pithy and futile aspirations, providing no absolution and no liberation. It only further enslaves.

I have arrived. This planet is all-too similar to the ones my feet have trod before. The Aeterium Axis have no moderator and no sense of challenge; they therefore prey upon the weak.

And weak men are here, these plebeians. These immaterial trifles. Including one in particular.

He is close now. I am supremely confident that this is the dark rock in space on which he is but a prisoner. *I feel him.* He is slave not only to his geography, but also now to the whims of the mercilessly callous and untouchably distant galactic sadists. The Aeterium Axis are such sadists, and I have never known worse.

This new hapless victim is no stronger nor weaker than I once was. Against his better judgment he is enslaved, doomed forever to tally the toll and hope in vanity that his petty fancies shall meet their inclinations.

Verily, he is in for a rude awakening.

One away or one to stay, and balance anew, the fool chants, echoing vainly with gravitas the false incantations of his overlords. He desires not the acclaim nor the esteem that

I did; proud humility that he bears. It shall not work out for his good; all such striving leads only to ego and self.

I smirk to myself as I gaze around. They call this Africa, do they? This land is crawling with organic lifeforms bound up in the fruitless pursuit of survival. Such elementary penchants. These land-locked creatures prowl around to entrap their prey, to rip it to shreds and feast upon its flesh.

And so shall I.

So shall I.

I shall need an Earth name, I fear. One in which I can blend in and so conduct my comings and goings without alerting him to my presence. And I choose -here I pause, taking in the signals of the millions of beings who have walked this Earth before me, perusing identities- ahh yes, this shall suffice:

Xavier Donovan.

Yes, I do enjoy the sound of that. It's melodic, though imperfect.

I lightly trace the circle of the medallion around my chest. It is all that I bear, yet it holds me in perfect form, carrying my essence, driving me, empowering unto me might beyond reason. Might which I shall use for my benefit and my eventual conquest.

This naked form I have elected for – save only the medallion around my neck – strides noiselessly across the plain, taking in the sights and sounds of all around me. I shall need clothing, that is for certain. I shall need to blend in. I tap my medallion, and am one with consciousness. The medallion glows, and from it emanates the familiar mist, hardening and coalescing into form, fanning out and blanketing my frail human shell with the chosen attire unique to talismans and those in the service of the Aeterium Axis.

Animals, naked unto themselves, study me with intrigue and fascination. Some of them stand and slowly trail me in my wake, presumably sizing me up for a meal. I shall disappear before they give chase. After all, one cannot overtake the wind, though one has four legs to my two.

One day, soon, I shall home in on his precise coordinates. The world has heard rumor of him, and that rumination has gone up like a klaxon into the multiverse, fanning out in desperate thirst for knowledge of The Iskander.

One, in particular, seeks to know him intimately, and I shall find her as well. I can feel it. I shall find her presently, and I shall kill her soundly.

No matter how long it takes, I shall find my targets. The Iskander – this wretched and pathetic slave unwittingly doing the bidding of the Aeterium Axis – is near, and my time is at hand. His blood shall be on my knife, and his essence shall fade under my stab.

And then, should he have been so clumsily fortunate as to have extended his line, I will have the great pleasure of hunting down his offspring. None shall remain. I will blot their memory from this cold rock.

I shall enjoy every minute of rending him to particulates of dust that float homeless for all eternity.

It shall be all dalliance and pleasure, all of it.

12 | RESCUE
June 14th 2062 · The Talisman

I'm here for business, not pleasure.

Lives are in danger, edging closer – ever closer – to the brink. Oblivious to their own peril, caught up in the bliss of the moment, they step further backward. There are a lot of them. My work is cut out for me.

First, I breathe. I lightly tap the medallion on my chest, infusing strength into my being and supernatural ability into my core. My suit glows and flickers, flashes and burns with blue heat. I feel the temperate air around me, gathering strength into my soul for the task ahead.

I inhale deeply.

There are thirty-two of them. This would be a huge score. I try not to think about that. That's always been the objective, but there is a purity here; a nobler ambition at play that is irrefutable and unavoidable. It's nearly always only been about the numbers, and I always know precisely where I stand. But this time, it's different. My heart is gripped.

Gripped by the little girl in the pure white dress holding a fluffy light brown teddy bear.

Gripped by the grandparents who outlived the gorgons and the Blockades and stuck around to watch their granddaughter tie the knot.

Gripped by the sweet music gracing the air around me, how it flows around them and serenades them, cradling their every move in its sonorous embrace.

And gripped, most of all, by the two of them. Man and wife, having freshly tied the knot, leaving and cleaving, becoming a new bond in their own right.

They stand together now, gazing endearingly into each other's eyes while the photographer instructs. They are nearly oblivious to the universe's presence around them, knowing only each other and their blossoming love.

And right then, my heart pangs with pain. Pain and remorse, knowing full well what they feel, having tasted and drunk deeply of the emotion swelling through them at this very moment. The tears build inside me as I yearn for days past: to a time where I was deeply in love with my new wife.

On the day of our ceremony, I loved her the *least*. That love only grew more and more as we spent our lives together. As we created life, entwined in the embrace of only us. As we swooned, fell, and were caught by the only one meant to catch us.

My sweet Janine, I weep softly to myself, *how I've failed you. But I will reclaim you - I promise,* I silently vow. And with that, I'm jerked back to awareness.

A portion of the rock crumbles underneath them. I've grieved too long.

Several of them go over. Their rate of descent will vary for each of them depending on their body mass and initial burst of velocity times gravity. Computations run through me for each of them, assessing their predicted mass and projected path.

All of them exclaim in agonized surprise, as their bodies start to plummet over the cliff overlooking the sunset. The orange orb in the sky cares nothing for their plight; it watches the tragedy unfold silently.

But I don't.

At that precise moment, I'm ripping a funnel through the air, clutching as many of them as I can, darting back up to the cliff repeatedly to drop them off. In rapid zig-zag succession, leaving only a blue vapor trail in my wake, I'm tearing up and down the cliff face.

The little girl is jolted in surprise as I fetch her just as her body nearly shatters on the sharp outcropping of rocks below. I stare into her frightened eyes as her stomach reels. The teddy bear drops from her grip and she shrieks, wailing, jolted from her current position and instantaneously rematerializing atop the cliff.

Debris, dust, rocks and earth rain down upon all of them in a shower of earth-filled frenzy.

She is back on the cliff, and I go for the next.

And the next.

And the next.

I'm nearly spent, but I gather all thirty-one of them. They're all safe! Bewildered and shell-shocked, but safe. All of them.

All thirty-one of them.

And panic sets in. Not just in them, for whom this day has nearly taken a frightening and fatal turn.

Also for me.

I count them. They're all there… aren't they?

A high-pitched wail of shuddering agony.

Fingers pointing. Arms outstretched, reaching downward. I don't get it. What's the problem?

All thirty-*one* of them.

Oh no, I silently mourn. I've missed one. Who did I miss? My face scans the crowd. I see the bride-

One to stay…

The groom. The groom! Where is the groom?

One away…

I zoom back to the rocks below, and suddenly I'm there, surveying the bloodshed, visually taking in the carnage of a body broken well before its time.

There lies the groom, shattered against the rocks, his midsection impaled on a coral-encrusted pinnacle, his intestines spilling out, face frozen in catatonic disbelief.

Horror seizes me, and I gasp in frustration.

One away.

Balance anew?

Where is the balance in this?

Why did this poor man have to die on the cusp of bliss? A life deprived of utter joy at its very apex of potential.

There's nothing to do but weep for him. I move, clutching his rent and tattered body. The blood flows through the waves and onto my suit, encompassing me.

I take him into my arms.

We're back on the cliff. I gently lay him down.

The entire crowd continues to gape down below, their jaws elongated, their eyes wide with disbelief. Screams of panic and alarm. They don't see him anymore.

They will, once they turn back around.

I'm unable to contain my grief for him. What is all this new emotion seizing me? A whimper escapes my lips as I leave him there, reluctantly dropping precious trinkets in my wake. They will doubtless resound gratitude for the lives saved; but she will now have a forever ache that no amount of gold talismans can assuage.

And now I'm preparing to disappear into the void and reappear back home in Olympia, mourning, mourning, mourning, just as they are doing in Princeville, Kauai.

One away, or one to stay...

Where is the balance?

A tiny stuffed bear floats away on the tide, ripped from its owner, soggy and sinking down to the depths.

What am I even doing here? He should have been saved, to be with his bride.

Eight hundred eighty saved. That's one hundred twenty to go. But it should be eight hundred eighty-one.

It *should* be one hundred nineteen.

I have failed them.

That bride will have to live without her groom. I am bound to her in that respect; this groom – me – will have to live without his bride. But, for her, there's no way for me to bring him back. That was never part of her agreement. He died, just as I once did.

And now, I'm stuck in hollowed-out rumination.

I'm here for mourning, and nothing else.

Part Two:
Intensity Rising

13 | QUESTIONS
JUNE 16ᵀᴴ 2062 · ONYX SLEATER

I don't know where he is, and I wish I did.

He hasn't reappeared for two days now, but I've heard rumors.

My mind is endlessly spinning over what he said. I sit here at my desk chasing rabbit trails. He's a Dark Ghost once more… evading my nose, dodging my searches, staying just out of the glare of my searchlight.

He keeps to the shadows, just like a ghost.

A Dark Ghost. I think I liked that name better. Better than Talisman… maybe even better than 'Liam.'

I think this Talisman, however, may have slipped up. Liam – if that's even really his name – might think that I'm not that sharp, or he might think me too inattentive or negligent to catch the inadvertent bread crumbs he's left behind.

But I *did* catch them. That's what I do.

August 4ᵗʰ, 2057.

Kentucky.

Flint Ridge Road.

Jet.

Wife died by gorgon.

Blue – something.

He didn't say his wife's name; smart move on his part. That would be easy to put two and two together. But she obviously died on August 4ᵗʰ somewhere in Kentucky on Flint Ridge Road. And this 'Jetzenburg' guy he mentioned: I don't know who that is, but I'll find him as well.

So far, however… nothing.

I go to see Brent. He's sitting in his office with his feet up on his desk, poring over the quarterly subscriber report. "Anything?" he asks.

"Not yet. Still searching."

He holds up the trinket I dropped off for him after my first meeting with The Talisman.

"Liam, huh?" Brent asks sardonically. "Can't be that hard to find, especially with the reduced population. It's only been two decades. We've had, what, maybe fifteen to twenty-million new souls born on average each year since liberation. That's three hundred forty million since then. Can't be that many named 'Liam' in that batch."

"Yeah, but he's older than that, Chief," I remind him. "He's gotta be pushing forty. Late thirties at least."

"You buy his cockamamie UFO story?"

I shrug. "Who knows? With what we've all seen down here since 2026, who the heck knows, Brent? I mean, anything's possible, right? The gorgons showed us that there are things out there beyond our control; things that want to toy with us. Earth seems to be everyone's playground but our own. It's someone else's sandbox now. We're just maybe the irritating fly that gets in their way. The gorgs swatted us hard… twice."

He nods, cocking an eyebrow, still ogling the talisman I gave him. "Sure is pretty, isn't it? Strange as heck, but pretty. Same stuff as last time."

"The usual suspects? Iron, nickel, palladium?"

He nods again. "Yep. Magnesium, iridium, cobalt, gold. But three particular elements not to be found on the periodic table. As before."

I shake my head and sigh. "He gave me what he gave me. In time, he'll cough up the rest. He wants to tell his story, Chief. I can feel it. There's just-" I end, lamely.

Brent turns to me. "Just what?"

"Just," I start, "well, since we're speaking of elements, there's the added element of danger. Chief, I've seen this guy dematerialize right before my eyes more than once now. Right down at 13th and L during the attack. He just vanished right in front of me. Then he did it three more times in my apartment. I'm not crazy, I *saw* it. Teleporter. And that suit…"

"What about the suit?"

"It's got… powers. Or… something. I dunno," I said, shaking my head and sighing again. "Everything he's said so far attests to the fact that there's something else out there yet again. I don't think this guy wanted any of it to happen. It sounds like he just got caught up in it accidentally. Bad luck, and they kicked him when he was down. Think of what he told me about the curse they laid on him."

"Who is *they*?"

"Yeah. Well, that's the part no one likes. The aliens – or Martians – or galactic nincompoops, whoever the heck they are. They say he's got to complete his mission."

"Of saving all those lives."

"Yeah. And he's close, Brent. You heard about that wedding in Hawaii two days ago? That's when he vanished. Right in front of me. Then we get the international wire and hear about a wedding party. A cliff. The cliff gives way, thirty-two people plummet to their death."

"Only they don't die. Mr. Liam Ghost Guy swoops in and saves them all!" Brent opines, stretching his arms out in grandiose and theatrical aplomb.

"Not all of them. The groom died, remember. He missed it. I think Liam's out there, feeling guilty. He's got to be. You would be too. Heck, I would feel bad. But think about it: he told me he was up to eight hundred forty-nine lives saved. Now he's up to eight eighty. He's got one hundred twenty to go."

"And then what? He gets his wife back? I'd have to see it to believe it. Someone's messing with this guy."

"Ever the Doubting Thomas, Chief," I say, clicking my tongue. "Is it so far-fetched? I mean, he's supernatural. Or, at least his *suit* is. Is it so outside the realm of possibility to believe that if they can grant him foresight and teleportation ability – and God knows what else – that they can bring back a life as well?"

Brent says nothing, just stares, glowering, at the talisman he's holding.

"Chief?"

"Keep searching. You're good at it. You'll find him. And mark my words, it sounds like he might have a twinkle in his eye for you, Onyx." Brent looks at me slyly.

Now it's my turn to cock an eyebrow. "He'd be a fool not to," I say, and then we both break into a grin.

It's 6:09pm. I really need to get back home. Part of me wants to, because I know he knows where I live, but I realize he also knows where I work, and he could instantly show up anywhere he wanted to if he was so inclined. So there's no point in being here nor there. The computers are faster here anyway, so I stay.

He's probably watching me as we speak.

I've got Chrome open. Searching. I type in as many queries as I can.

August 4ᵗʰ 2057, Kentucky. My eyes scan down the page. Nothing remarkable pulls up.

Liam + wife died by gorgon.

Scanning. Nothing concrete. Far too many results to zero in on. Have to run it through a filter for this. Far too many Liams died – and their wives – when eighty-five percent of the world's population got wiped out. Nothing solid there either. Olivia and Liam were still two of the most popular names around the time of the gorgons. There are – or *were* – a ton of Liams out there.

Kentucky, Jetzenburg.

Scrolling. Scrolling. Nothing.

Jetzenburg. Flint Ridge Road. August 2057.

Nothing.

I sigh, running my fingers through my hair and staring at the screen. I take a sip of my frigid coffee. It's revolting, and my scowl attests to it.

I stare at the screen, briefly wondering to myself if he lied about the date. He wants to protect me. He wants to protect himself. He has a mission, and he's close to fulfilling it. So what would he do? Lie. Cover up. Just to throw me off.

Think, Onyx. Think.

"Night, Sleater," a voice calls out. It's Brent. He's going home for the night. "You leaving soon?"

"Yeah," I reply tiredly. "Just… still trying to catch a ghost. You know me. Tightening the noose." I offer a fatigued smile.

"Yeah, well, doesn't sound like a noose would hold a ghost anyway," my editor replies with a note of apathetic resignation, strolling slowly over to me. He places an encouraging hand on my shoulder. "Maybe *loosen* the noose a bit and give him a chance. Zoom out a bit. Widen your search." My editor casually places my talisman on the desk in front of me, tapping it with his finger. "I'll see you tomorrow."

I wave to him. "Later."

I turn back to the screen, exhaling loudly. I'm so close to the monitor that it momentarily fogs. There are Kleenex on my desk; I reach out for one to wipe off the screen and restore clarity.

And then I stop.

Noose. Tightening. No. *Loosening.* Maybe Brent has a point?

If I were trying to throw someone a bone, I'd throw them a small one first. I wouldn't be so precise. But what if he was throwing me a precise bone, but the *wrong* one, in order to throw me off?

He *did* lie to me. I know it.

I search.

Kentucky. Flint Ridge Road. I can't remember precisely where he said. He definitely said Kentucky and Flint Ridge Road.

Results pour in. I pull up a map, zooming out and seeing more of the land. To the southwest, I spot something that rings a bell.

Mammoth Cave National Park Visitor Center.

Something clicks. *Mammoth Cave.* Wasn't there a Blockade there, a big one? I grew up in the one in DC, but I remembered some of the other names around the country. Mammoth Cave housed the original leader of the resistance, Vance Cardona... the eventual President of the United States of America, succeeding the deplorable Jean Graham.

I stick a pin in the digital map near Mammoth Cave. Flint Ridge Road runs east and west for a few miles, changing names here and there, ending up at Mammoth Cave. And he said Blue – *something.*

My heart starts pounding with excitement.

I'm closing in on you, Liam.

So: something happened around Mammoth Cave. Hmm. I type in my next search. *Mammoth Cave + August 2057.* I intentionally leave out the '4th' of August to widen my search.

Various results spill in. Artifacts of cleanup and rebuilding from the cave and the Blockade there. Articles scroll by me. One catches my eye.

Investigation Ongoing For Bizarre Light Show Following Mammoth Cave Tragedy.

Tragedy?

My eyes squint as I click on it. It's the Bowling Green Daily News from August 12th, 2057:

The investigation continues regarding a strange sighting outside Cave Creek nine nights ago.

Area eyewitnesses remember seeing lights descend from the sky in the area to the northeast of Mammoth Cave on the evening of August 3rd following the continuing renovation and cleanup of the Mammoth Cave Blockade DN312.

Many will remember Mammoth Cave was one of the original Blockades prepared in defense of the gorgon invasion of 2026, and the commanding officer there was none other than future President Vance Cardona.

Several eyewitnesses report seeing two small patterns of light zip back up into the sky early in the morning of August 4th. It is unconfirmed as of yet what they were, but various accounts report that they may have simply been optical illusions considering the ideal view of the Milky Way Galaxy and stellar patterns due to minimal light pollution given its position as an International Dark Sky Park.

I continue to scroll, and something catches my eye. My heart races.

There was some concern that these accounts may in fact corroborate the reported August 3rd death of an infantry member rumored to have been temporarily stationed at Mammoth Cave. The victim, a female, has not yet been identified, but an informant who wishes to remain anonymous has identified her as the wife of a high-ranking infantry member.

It has been confirmed that two of those members are in fact the very two who served in the Atlantic Ocean Liberation that took place in December 2042, as well as served with the President and Chief of Staff Monzon during the 2045 return of the gorgons. Captain Cameron 'Jet' Shipley and Corporal Liam 'Foxy' Mayfield of Blue Spring,

Kentucky... Speculation is now rampant that this deceased female may in fact be the wife of Corporal Mayfield and in fact the daughter of former President Vance Cardona.

I stop. A chill runs down the entire length of my body. I reread the article.

A dead woman.

Corporal Liam 'Foxy' Mayfield of Blue Spring, Kentucky. Blue *Spring, Kentucky,* I realize, amazed.

And 'Jet' Shipley!

Not Jetzenburg! *Jet! Jet Shipley,* the Captain in the wars who lost his brother and was virtually tied at the hip with Liam 'Foxy' Mayfield!

Liam Fox Mayfield! 'Foxy,' as he was known. The son-in-law to President Vance Cardona!

My fingers are shaking. I take a deep breath. What was Cardona's daughter's name? It started with a J. *Think, Onyx.*

I google it. *'President Vance Cardona and wife Andi's daughter.'*

The results scroll down the screen.

Janine Marie Pullman Mayfield.

President's Daughter Confirmed Killed August 3rd 2057 by Rogue Gorgon.

Mammoth Cave Tragedy Claims First Daughter.

Blue Spring's Own Corporal Liam 'Fox' Mayfield Devastated Following Wife's Death By Gorgon.

Corporal Mayfield MIA Since Wife's Death.

Popular War Corporal Liam Mayfield MIA Off Job Corps / Flint Ridge Road.

President And First Lady In Mourning.

August 3rd 2057 Death of President's Daughter Coincides With Strange Nighttime Visitors.

Blue Spring KY Corporal Loses Wife To Gorgon.

I sit back in my chair, panting, near tears.

Liam – The Talisman – *Liam,* I think, struggling – is none other than Corporal Liam Fox Mayfield, the war hero!

I lean back in and resume my search.

Liam Fox Mayfield + Janine Cardona Wedding.

The results bathe the screen. I only need the first one. It's right there. I know it.

Gorgon War Hero marries First Daughter in Stirring Ceremony.

I click on it.

And there it is. I nearly choke. There's the picture of the two of them. He in his black tux, she in her white dress, newlyweds gazing giddily into the camera. I zoom in.

Those eyes. I see them instantly. Through his blonde locks – I remember seeing other photos of him and Jet following the war in 2045, where his head was shaved – I can see his eyes. He and Janine look so happy together.

It's him.

Liam 'Foxy' Mayfield is The Talisman.

I put my hands to my mouth.

I've found him.

I've loosened the noose and widened the net, and I've found him. I'm shaking all over. *Breathe, Onyx. Just breathe. You've cracked it. Compose yourself.*

I try. But it's too much.

I rip my phone to my ear and call Brent immediately. I've got to see Liam again, and I've got to see him now. *But how?!*

Help me find him, I pray to whoever's listening.

A depressed sigh wells up and out of me.

He knows where to find me, and I wish he would.

14 | DILEMMA
June 19th 2062 · The Talisman

I'm stuck, and I can't unstick myself.

The last salvations – they were drudgery. I knew they were going to happen, and it's not every day you catch three people having sex when a burglar breaks in. I saved a threesome and killed the bad guy. Broke his neck.

Trouble is, it was a man cheating on his wife with two neighborhood women in her Bible book club. Awful.

Despicable. I didn't want to save any of them, but I did it. It was awkward beyond belief, and I just went through the motions. I cast them an angry glare as I left, almost unwilling to leave them their talismans. In my heart, I know they're answerable to God, not me. He'll pronounce judgment… if He even still exists. Maybe the Aeterium Axis is using someone else to bring Him back as well, I muse, grimly.

Eight hundred eighty-two now. I've got one hundred eighteen to go.

One away or one to stay, and balance anew.

Whatever. Sometimes, this curse sucks. They can't all be noble and clean, antiseptic and honorable, right? I have to save the deserving *and* the undeserving. But this one stings given what happened to that poor groom. Surely, *he* was deserving.

I missed him. How could I miss him?

I don't feel like returning to Onyx. She's out there, and every look at her – no matter how brief or passing – reminds me of my beloved Janine Marie. Every single one. Dare I tell her this? Dare I confess and divulge?

I want to see her again, I honestly do, but I can't bring myself to do it in this state. Grief enshrouds me like a cloak, and I want to hide in it and avoid this cold, dark world with its impurities; its demands; its constant need of rescue.

My belief in God has taken a hit. I admit it. If there is a God, where is He? Why doesn't He intervene? Why hasn't He? Surely saving people is *His* purview, not mine. This irritating burden placed squarely on me by virtue of a simple walk of grief one dark night in Kentucky… how it weighs me down.

I'm so close now. *So* close. I can't abandon it. I've always known that. They offered it to me, and I didn't say no. *I should have said no.* It's cost me my relationship with my sons. No, no, that's not fair to them. *I* cost me my relationship with them by taking Janine on mission with me. I never should have.

The Aeterium Axis stated clearly what it would cost, and what I had to do. I will never forget it.

One thousand souls saved, and your wife is returned to you, they said. *Fall short, fail, lose the medallion or abandon your obligation, and your lost love stays dead. But not only that, Iskander,* they said, *someone else shall perish as well.*

No pressure, right? I can always resume my mission, but the lives saved quota doubles as a penalty, and now there would be *another* beloved soul dead.

They made me swear to them. At the time, I thought it achievable. But as I draw near, the dread in my heart grows ever deeper and more tangible. Will they keep their word? Do they *really* have the power to do what they've promised?

In my heart, I know that either one of my sons… or Onyx… is next. It *might* be Wayne Trudeau, but I doubt it. He's not nearly as precious to me. No. It'll be my boys… or Onyx will be the next one I'll lose. They know it, and so do I. I never should have brought them or her into this. I never should have thrown Onyx a bone, because now she's caught up in this tempest with me, and the nearer I draw to the fulfillment of my oath, the more the danger becomes ever graver.

But if I know anything about Onyx – and her journalistic ways – she won't go quietly into the night.

She's drawn to me, and she won't remove herself.

15 | CONTACT
June 19th 2062 · The Zorander

It shall be my first contact with an Earth person.

I have just departed the road, labeled with intermittent signs declaring 'Allatoona Gtwy.' Now, here, at this sullen and dejected corner, I find a small blue building labeled 'Collins Corner.' Various small metal craft are stationed throughout; one of them is positioned directly underneath some vast overhang, and they appear to be conveying a liquid into their craft while they survey a kind of terminal. Most of them are small, moving to and fro on wheels, emitting a light rumble. Others are larger and are far more obstreperous. One such weighty craft departs towing a formidably-sized trailer of some type, ejecting a fiercely gray pollutant into the air in its wake. Revoltingly impure.

There is one. He appears to be an elderly male. I behold the frail human, nonchalantly taking the air to the north outside this small outlet, apparently a waypoint for goods and merchandise. He is imbibing an unknown substance out of a bottle and inhaling a mist-like white vapor emitting from a small staff. He is positioned to the south of the establishment, leaning against a large concrete mass.

The human is clad in a multi-hued square-patterned shirt tucked into blue clothlike fabric at the waist, connected with a large sash with a solid gold promenade at the front. He is crowned with a wide hat sporting a dimple at its peak.

"Greetings," I bid. He turns to me, unaware of my approach. He nods, lightly pinching the brim of his hat and briefly nudging it down.

"Evenin,'" he replies. "Help you?"

Strange. His language is curiously abbreviated.

"Evenin,'" I reply in turn, adopting his staccato manner of speech. "My name Xavier Donovan. New to this domain," I say, preserving the crude, cut-off manner of speech and manufacturing a warm smile. That is, after all, a strange connection point between these lowly humans.

The elderly male watches me curiously, studying me up and down. He slowly, steadily sucks on the small staff, preserves the smoke inside him somehow, and then breathes it out in a long plume while nearly laughing, "Boy, ain't that the truth. Yer from some stage play, right? In a musical? Not from these parts?" He snaps his fingers irritatingly beneath this nose of mine.

"These parts," I say, cocking my head. I do not know where 'these parts' are. "Please enlighten my essence."

His eyes squint, and then he erupts into sudden laughter. I find this abrupt change in emotion jarring and unbefitting our conversation. I am here for information, after all, not scorn. "Your essence!" he cries amidst laughter. "Oh my. And you in Acworth, Georgia, ah-mee-go!" he laughs again. "Where the heck you from?"

"The knowledge of my origin is not critical for your cognizance, subcreature," I say to him. His smile fades as he appears to struggle with the meaning of what I have said. Perhaps I was overly multisyllabic for his mundane thought patterns. "I am looking for a stranger."

He sneers and looks away. "Crap. Go look in any mirror, friend. Ha!" He erupts into newfound laughter, turning away from me and continuing to imbibe his drink amidst his amusement.

Xavier Donovan's attire is no doubt alien to this human, and I am unacquainted with this region, to be sure. Nevertheless, now I know which region I am in. *Acworth, Georgia,* the human reported. I have my bearings. Now, all that remains is to locate my target. He is close. There must be rumor of him.

"I am in need of an information source so that I might locate someone. Where would I find such a source?" I inquire of him.

"Ha! You not only from somewhere else, friend, you must be livin' in the dark ages. Y'all buzz off, now." He does not turn my way, but keeps his back to me, ignoring.

The human pulls out a small rectangular device from his pocket and absorbs himself in it, balancing the tip of his bottle and the smoke staff in one hand, while staring at the small glowing device with his left. He occasionally chuckles to himself while shaking his head in incredulity at me. But he appears to be looking for something on the small device. Perhaps it is a peripheral of some kind? Perhaps it is a window into the information that I seek.

"What is that which you hold there?" I ask.

The human exhales noisily and rolls his head. "Look, *friend*," he says, rotating toward me with an annoyed expression. He begins to slowly pace toward me. "You's clearly some kind of freak. I done told you to buzz off. Hit the road, chump," he says, and then he ejects pasty fluid from his oral cavity, sloppily, onto my left shoe.

I have what I need.

"Thank you," I say, and then I place my right hand on his left shoulder. Connection made.

The man freezes, staring at me. His mouth drops open, and he emits a low, nearly inaudible moan as I extract his life force. I observe, silently, as his cheeks become sallow, and the whites of his eyes take on a blackened hue, the color of the afterlife. They crumple, their remains retreating inside the elderly man's skull. His hat, once form-fitting to his head, loses its positioning and slides down the withering, steaming stump that was his cranium.

I watch him, breathing in his fading essence, utterly entertained. His intestines, his heart, his lungs, his organs, all of them, reduced to vapor which I gratefully inhale.

The man's flesh, already gritty and coarse with age, becomes dry and cracked as the bottle falls from his hand. There is a label across the midsection of it. *Bacardi Rum.* The smoke stick drops in the midst of the splashed liquor and shattered glass, and it ignites. The man begins to be consumed from the feet up by the flickering flames.

I smile at him as I retrieve the rectangular device from his hand and step backward. Two fingers disconnect from his hand and melt in their decay as I do so. I turn away from the dying human, device in hand, and dematerialize, leaving a smoking, fading husk where he once stood.

As I suspected, the device proves to be some form of search peripheral. It is similar to our own peripherals for inquests, though crude and restricted, bound to this small form. Doubtless it was constrained to this infinitesimal rectangular shape so as to fit in the hands of these puny humans.

Learning the process of forming the letters and syntax in search strings does not take me long. I am soon searching for rumor of a ghost… a mystery… an enigma.

Searching for the one whom I know is close. He is here, and it shall not be long before I find him.

Strange – that elderly human's death was intriguing. Pleasurable. I have not killed in such a manner before, but of all my victims, that one was particularly quaint and enjoyable. I hope soon to be able to repeat the process with another hapless victim. I hope to be able to repeat it with The Iskander himself.

Directing scorn was never the correct approach for the elderly male, and had he any idea of my true identity, my calling, my very *power*, he would have treated me with the respect and honor that I am due.

For I am The Zorander, and I bring balance.

I continue my search. The tiny device has scant references to mysteries and strange occurrences that this planet refers to as anomalies or extraterrestrial events. At some point or another, this tiny rock in space has been subjected to various atrocities and other dooms. I find the results enjoyable to read, as it strikes me that they deserve their misfortune more than they know.

A planet acquainted with misery would be exactly the place for the Aeterium Axis to call upon for balance, in all of their enriched sadism. Exactly the type of environment these cosmic killjoys' and taskmasters' cruel and callous enforcement would take great pleasure in binding such victims to their insidious chore.

It matters not. I am here. I shall find The Iskander, one way or another, and the time draws near for a great balancing of the scales in my favor. The Aeterium Axis cannot exist forever, and once I deprive them of their envoy,

I will trace their signal back to their own location, at which point I shall deprive them of their life.

It shall be my final contact with anyone.

16 | CONVERSATIONS
JUNE 20TH 2062 · ONYX SLEATER

Time passes with no sign of him.

It's late on a Tuesday night, and I'm still reeling.

Liam Fox Mayfield is the Talisman, and the Talisman is out there somewhere. He truly is a dark ghost, and the more he continues to evade me, the more I yearn for his return.

I find myself at odd hours pleading into the void for his return, hoping against hope that *someone* will hear me and make it happen. I have no idea who I'm praying to, but I'm trusting that someone hears me. Perhaps the same cosmic force that visited him in the first place. I don't know.

There's another thing. I can't help but feel sorry for him regarding the loss of his wife. *Janine*. To lose a spouse must be devastating. I wouldn't know. But then I did a greater deep-dive for pictures.

I found myself looking at a doppelganger. I didn't notice it at first in her wedding photos; she was so dolled up. But it's unmistakable. She looks so much like me.

The resemblance is uncanny, and I wonder if that's part of the draw. I wonder if there's anything in his psyche; anything as far as a predilection for me in particular. The truth stares me in the face: she's nearly a twin.

Janine Marie Pullman Mayfield. The daughter of President Vance Cardona. I wonder how the former President feels about him. Surely, a little investigative reporting wouldn't hurt anyone.

Surely, the former President of the United States of America wouldn't mind a call from a reporter. It's late, but he's in the same time zone, at least, having retired down in Florida.

I take a deep breath, and grab my phone.

"Please, this is important," I say. His aide won't hear me. Jesse Garrison used to be a Secret Service Agent under Cardona, continuing on at the pleasure of the president. I read that he was in the Presidential Emergency Operations Center during the gorgons' second wave in 2045, as well as the fact that he and other agents staved off a human incursion into the PEOC. He was loyal then, and he is loyal now. And today, he's trying to turn me away, despite my pleas.

My stomach is in real, tangible knots as I make my case to him. "Mr. Garrison, I-"

"Ms. Sleater, " he interrupts me, "the President doesn't wish to discuss Mr. Mayfield any longer. Now if you don't mind-"

"Mr. Garrison, *please. Please* don't hang up, I beg you. I'm not calling to pester the former President. This is a matter of family. Something has happened to Mr. Mayfield, and I think the President would appreciate knowing the fate of the father of his grandchildren."

An awkward pause while he assesses this cryptic disclosure. "*What* has happened, Ms. Sleater? I will relay the message."

"Please do so. My number should be on your caller ID, or you can reach me through The Post."

"I'd like to know *now*, please, so that I can relay it to him direct-"

"I appreciate it, Mr. Garrison. Thank you for your time. If the President would like to know, I'll be available."

"Wait-"

I hang up on him. Hopefully, I've planted enough of a seed of curiosity in his mind, and he's contractually obligated to relay my message anyway. I can't fault him for wanting to shield Cardona – after all the former President is now in his seventies, and his wife remains in a state of constant mourning after losing their daughter. Despite all of that, in my heart I believe he would want to know.

So now, the waiting game begins.

Will I get in touch with Liam again before Cardona gets in touch with me? We'll see.

My hand doesn't let go of my phone. I'm clutching it to my chest. I *do* want to protect Liam. He said that individuals can't know he's here. He said they can't know who he is.

You're playing a dangerous game, Onyx, I whisper to myself, taking a deep breath.

I want to protect him, and I silently vow to do just that. I'll try not to reveal anything about Mayfield's supernatural mission or what he's been doing. But I am going to find out what I can from the President about the Talisman's state of mind, what happened that led up to his daughter's death, and how I might be able to get in touch with him again.

Because that, honestly, is what I want right now more than anything.

JUNE 21ST 2062

Ringing. Endless ringing, permeating my dreams. I toss about on my bed, hair all askew and drifting into my mouth. I should have pinned it like I always do before bed. Too much on my mind. What is that damn ringing?

My phone. I had forgotten I changed the ringtone, and now it's repeatedly ringing. "Alexa, turn on the bedroom light," I say. She does so. My eyes wince from the change.

I turn over and grab it just as it stops, and I'm squinting. *Wow*, I muse, *I must have downed a few more Stroh's last night and conked out.*

I look hard at the number. Seven missed calls from a 305 area code. *The Florida Keys.* Where former President Vance Cardona retired with his wife.

I swallow nervously, and my stomach is revisited by those same knots that made themselves known during Garrison's call.

This is not the same number I programmed into my phone for Jesse Garrison, his aide. No. This is Cardona's number himself, either a landline or a cell, and he's calling me personally. Either he or his wife, I think.

I take a deep breath, and sit up with the shock of it. My phone reads 1:32 AM. For a moment, my brain reverts to military time; it wasn't so long ago where I was scurrying about through the walls of our DC Blockade and every single clock displayed *only* military time. It was nice to revert back to regular hours.

However you slice it, it's early.

No rest for the weary.

He's obviously awake – or she is – so there's no harm in returning the call. He must understand that I was sleeping as well, so I'm sure he'll be sympathetic.

Am I assuming too much?

I take a deep breath to gather my senses, run my hands through my hair to sweep it back, and focus, tapping the number.

In a moment, I'm greeted by a thick and husky New York accent. From everything I remember of him during his tenure, President Cardona is gritty, gruff, determined, stoic, staunch, and every bit the leader that we all needed to get us through two devastating alien invasions.

I don't know what has happened to him in the seventeen years since our liberation, but I did cover him in a series of articles a few years back – they weren't especially flattering. One of them actually dared to mention the loss of his daughter and I strayed too far in suggesting that her Secret Service detail left her to the whims of warriors; they should have protected her, and they failed in their charge. That's probably why Garrison doesn't like me; he is, after all, Secret Service, and now heads up Cardona's current security detail.

"Ms. Sleater," says the voice. It's unmistakably Cardona. "Thank you for calling me back."

"Mr. President, thank you for calling *me* back. I wasn't sure I was going to make it past Cerberus," I jest, meaning Garrison.

Cardona chuckles grimly. "Garrison is a very good man. He's no Cerberus; he just does his job. Now," he clears his throat, "I apologize for the lateness – or earliness – of the hour, but my curiosity got the better of me, and your message sounded urgent. At least that's what Cerberus reported to me."

My turn to chuckle.

"Indeed. Thank you, Mr. President. I've been weighing this out, and I don't really truly know how to broach this with you-"

"How about very carefully and concisely?"

I swallow again. He's an intimidating force, even over a phone call. President Vance Brennan Cardona, is, after all, the very figurehead of the resistance that struck back at the gorgons and also spearheaded the deposition of President Jean Graham, his wicked predecessor. The lady was going to actually nuke Iran, China and North Korea out of spite, under the pretense of destroying the gorgons. Sure, she herself positioned a massive counterattack that saw the gorgons' ultimate demise, but it was Cardona who was ultimately given the credit, whereas she was given the firing squad, not the least for murdering her Vice President, Eric Cooper.

Ancient history, I think to myself.

"Yes, Mr. President." A swell of courage shoots through me. I have a job to do, after all, and I'm just trying to do it. "I don't mean to intrude, and with all sensitivity, I have some information on your son-in-law, Liam Mayfield."

No response except presumably indignant silence.

"I-" I start, slowly, "I realize that he's an object of frustration and regret, no doubt. I've read what happened with your daughter and the incident at Mammoth Cave, sir.

But there have been recent developments that you may wish to consider."

He waits. "Such as?"

"Such as new revelations as to what has happened to him and-"

"Cut to the chase, Ms. Sleater. Please. Is my son-in-law alive?"

Curious that he should call Liam his son-in-law, given what I've heard about his resentment toward him. "Yes, sir, he is. Well, at least he *was*, as of two days ago. But-," I stammer, "something has happened. Something I think that he has not revealed to you, or his war buddy Jet Shipley, or perhaps anyone else, sir. Something that, I truly believe, was outside of his control."

Again, silence.

The President takes a deep, weary sigh, reflective of the time of day, and follows it with another pause. "Ms. Sleater, are you in Washington, DC, still?"

"Uh, yessir?"

"Any plans tomorrow?"

"Uh, no, not really, sir."

"I'll come see you at The Post."

I'm taken aback by this. Custom and tradition would usually see *me* traveling to *him* on The Washington Post's dime. But maybe he has other things in mind and wishes to speak personally, and perhaps away from Mrs. Cardona.

Either way, I'll be meeting the President. A thrill runs through me with nervous apprehension.

"Wow, I-" I stammer, again, "uh, okay, sir, I-"

"Ms. Sleater?"

I clear my throat. "No! It's fine. Totally fine. That would be welcome, sir. I'll be here. This is my personal cell." I appreciate the gesture, but perhaps I should at least offer the reverse, out of respect for him. "Are you sure you wouldn't like me to come to you? After all you've done for the country – and the world – it's the least I can do."

The man is a master of awkward pauses.

"No. I've stayed in caves long enough."

I understand his meaning.

But I also don't.

I'm not sure when I got back to sleep, but adrenaline kicks me into overdrive when the alarm sounds at 0600 hours – 6am, I correct myself – and I quickly shower and get myself ready to walk to the Post.

Thankfully, insurance is operational again, but my car is declared a total loss from the bank robbery kerfuffle. I'll have money for a new one soon. *Maybe I'll get a jet black Chevy Camaro,* I joke to myself. For now, I'm still walking to The Post.

Brent confirms that he's received a call from Cardona's security detail that he'll be arriving at Ronald Reagan at 12:30pm. He'll be driven over in an SUV and taken securely into our garage.

As I head south, something strikes me funny. I'm almost to the intersection where the robbery occurred a few days ago, when I get the distinct sensation I'm being watched. I can't shake it.

My legs slow to a measured pace, as I slowly crane my neck up and to the left. I half-expect to see a cloud of residual vapor floating there, but there's nothing. He was there once; a sniper taking out an assailant in the intersection, before he saved a family in a sedan.

The Talisman.

Liam Fox Mayfield.

For a brief moment, I cover the area as much as I can, visually, for any trace of him. I don't see him, but that doesn't mean he isn't here. He's watching me. He's *always* watching me. I wonder, even now, if he knows I'm meeting with his father-in-law, the former President.

He knows things before they happen, sure enough, but does that include clandestine meetings, or only future atrocities?

He's not here, I resign myself with a sigh, and I continue south.

"Mr. President," I greet him, extending my hand. "So nice to finally meet you in person."

"Mr. President," Brent also greets him heartily. "Thank you so much for coming."

President Cardona has a brisk, firm handshake, and he leans into me. I think he's always done that. Whether it's the absence of a preferred space bubble or just his congenial way of connecting with you, I don't know. I've seen it in pictures and video since he took office, and he's seemingly always been that way. I take comfort in the fact that he genuinely wants to embrace his fellow man.

"My pleasure," he replies heartily. "As we say, 'fuhgeddaboudit.' Any chance to get out and see the world. I'd never actually been to The Washington Post in my years at DC. Nice here. Ms. Sleater, you were here in DC under General Carson, is that correct?"

I nod enthusiastically, memories creeping back over me. "Mm-hm, yessir. That man was a living legend. I was sorry to hear that he had passed. He definitely made his mark then as well as in our defense in the 2045 invasion. I'm sorry for the loss of your friend."

The President waves me down. "Everett Carson was my friend. He was a good man."

Brent wastes no time. "Uh, Mr. President, we've got the conference room ready. It's right this way." Cardona nods. In his wake, a tall man nods to me, but says nothing. His face doesn't exactly radiate approval, and it's then that I realize that's Jesse Garrison, Cardona's Secret Service head. We've never met, but his face confirms what I had earlier suspected: he has no love for me based on my story. *Oh well. Can't win 'em all.*

He passes me on the way to the conference room. At the door, Cardona spins on his heels and puts his hands up. "Ah, folks, I'd like to talk to Ms. Sleater alone please, if you don't mind. Even you, Mr. Chastain, Mr. Garrison. Perhaps you wouldn't mind waiting outside while we catch up here." It isn't a question. Garrison glances at Brent, and then me.

"Certainly, Mr. President," Brent says. "Agent Garrison, I can show you around a bit before they call us back?"

Garrison nods. "Sir," he confirms with Cardona.

It's just the two of us now. Cardona beckons me into the conference room. I smile as I walk past him, feeling strangely rather *his* employee and not Brent's. I wonder acutely if he sees Janine in me as Liam did. He's her *father*; I'm *sure* he does, I tell myself. He's probably just stowing it. Guarding his emotions. Something like that.

We both sit, him straight across from me at the large oak conference table. I can just make out Brent leading Garrison around the office. A few of our other reporters – there aren't many – gawk through the glass at us at intervals. It isn't every day that you have a President of the United States in your newspaper headquarters.

He sits and stares at me, his eyes half-closed, with a comfortable, knowing smile on his face. I say nothing, just register that he's lost in thought for a moment. I shift my head and raise my eyebrows in questioning.

He shakes his head suddenly. "You look so much like my Janine," he says, finally, confirming my hunch. "Or, how she would have looked at this age."

"Certainly not as stunning," I add quickly. "I found a few of their wedding photos. She was a gorgeous young woman, Mr. President."

He heaves a sigh and now nods. "Yes. Yes, she was. She looks a lot like her mother. If it were a lot like me, 'gorgeous' is not the word I would use."

We both chuckle together.

"You have some information on my son-in-law, I believe," he says warmly, cutting to the chase.

"I do. And I'm glad I could tell you to your face, Mr. President. Firstly, however, may I ask a question?"

His eyebrows raise, as does his chin.

"What do you know," -here I momentarily bite my lip, being cautious- "of the night the First Daughter died?"

Cardona shifts in his seat, glancing around, lost in memory. "Only what I had been told by those around her. Captain Shipley and others who were with Liam during the cleanup op at Mammoth Cave. The former First Lady and I were at home at the White House at the time."

"Mm-hmm." I pause. "Well, first of all, allow me to express two things. One, my deepest sympathies on your loss. I realize it was five years ago, but a wound like this must still take time to heal, and I can only imagine how a conversation like this must be like peeling off a bandage."

"Mrs. Cardona would agree with you. Andi is still in mourning to this day."

I nod. "I understand. And… secondly, sir, I-" -here my speech fails me; I'm unsure how to address the article I wrote up criticizing his Secret Service- "I want to offer a retraction on the article I wrote about your Secret Ser-"

He already knew where I was going. He holds up his hand as he bows and shakes his head. "There's no need, Ms. Sleater. You're a reporter. I get it. You were just doing your job, and she *should* have been more protected. The guys at the time felt she was in good hands, and she had Liam, Jet, everyone else with them. As you know, she herself was a tried and true warrior in my own Blockade, and she proved herself many times both at DN312 and at Wright-Pat following the former president's attacks. She was a fighter. They said she wouldn't go, but…," he trailed off, and a grim smile of remembrance crept over his lips as his eyes drifted away from me, consumed by memories. "She was truly a fighter," he reiterates quietly. "Do you know, she once made a journey of two-hundred thirteen miles from Wright-Pat to join us at Mammoth Cave? All that distance, with the constant threat of gorgs at any minute. She was a brave soul, my Janine."

"I believe you, sir. I'm still sorry. I just wanted to clear the air."

He returns his eyes to me. "Well, there's no need. At least with me. Jesse, that's another story. Good luck with Cerberus," he chuckles.

"Thank you, sir," I laugh. "Well, firstly, let me start off by saying that this is not something I had anticipated. And, frankly, I think it's turning into the biggest story in years, second only to the gorgon invasion and the wars. I mean that."

His head tilts and his eyes narrow.

"What I have to tell you won't be easy to hear, sir. I hardly believed it myself, but, over and over again, despite my best efforts to disprove it, I'm left with little choice other than to accept the truth."

"What truth, exactly, Ms. Sleater?"

I take a deep breath. "Here goes."

I lay it all out for him.

Slowly I recount for Cardona all the details of my run-ins with the Dark Ghost. He is already familiar with the rumors of him. I leave out a few of the supernatural details for now. One thing at a time, and I want to proceed realistically first.

I brief him on the times I've been saved by him.

The apartment fire.

The mugging.

My trip to Seattle.

The bank robbery and intersection attack.

I can read his face. It's not one coated in disbelief or confusion. It doesn't take the former leader of the Resistance long to put two and two together. I think he's clued into me by the time I've described the bank robbery. The man was, after all, an IT Security guy and a Navy Seal once, before majoring in covert ops and subterfuge. He almost singlehandedly, clandestinely, spearheaded the overthrow of the corrupt President Jean Graham, before ascending to the upper echelons of politics. Her unseating was his greatest achievement.

"The man you're talking about is Liam Mayfield," he says. It isn't a question.

I nod, slowly. "Yessir, that's correct. But there's more. Much more."

"Such as?" His face is a grim slate. I can't tell if he wants to hear more about my vigilante, or if he wants to hear more about his son-in-law. There are definitely two sides to The Talisman Liam Mayfield, and the President is now forced to reconcile the two, as I was once forced to.

As for me, I'm wondering if I'm betraying Liam.

I don't want to endanger him, and there is a certain nobility in what he's doing. But I feel the President must know. If there are people out to stop him, and he's survived this long, then he must be protected. Maybe the President can help him. Maybe the President would *want* to help his son-in-law.

"Sir, Liam Mayfield is no longer… just… *Liam Mayfield.*" Cardona frowns in a perplexed annoyance. His jaw is outlined. "The night that Janine – the First Daughter – died, sir, something happened to him. He told me himself. At first, I didn't believe him sir, uh, I just… chalked it up to an incurable case of the crazies. But I've seen him do things that have defied logic."

"What happened to him, Ms. Sleater?" He clearly wants me to get to the point.

I swallow hard. This is either going to be skeptically and reluctantly accepted, given where he's been and all he's seen… or it's going to go over like a lead balloon, and he's out of here.

"Mr. President, your son-in-law visited me and shared his story. He specifically said that he would be endangering me by doing so. There is someone out there looking for him, maybe more than one, I don't know. He said no one can know he's here."

"Why?"

"Because of what happened to him." *Okay, here goes,* I think. "Sir, on the night of your daughter's passing, Liam was on the road outside Mammoth Cave. He was consumed by grief."

"I've heard that report, yes."

"You haven't heard the rest."

"I heard he went missing."

"Yessir," I reply. "It's what happened after that, sir. He noticed something – something in the night sky. Something in the forest off the road outside Mammoth Cave, somewhere nearby. He said he came in contact with some kind of… 'craft…' there. Pulsating with light, drawing him in. He said it spoke with Janine's voice and offered him a choice."

"What choice?"

"Sir, whoever put that craft there – or whoever piloted it there – whatever – they're not from around here. They've sort of 'conscripted' him to their service. They specifically offered to *resurrect* his wife, sir… in exchange for one thousand souls saved."

The President just stares at me, his brow furrowed, his mouth open in amazement.

"I know it sounds absurd, sir, but they're – again, whoever *they* are – obsessed with balance. He has this, this, mantra, this saying or something: *one away, or one to stay, and balance anew.* He has to save lives, and shield one thousand from death in order to usher your daughter back to life. That has been his mission ever since your daughter died, sir. They gave him some kind of special suit, and a medallion around his neck, and every time he goes and saves someone, he leaves these 'talisman' trinkets behind. I don't really know if that's by his choice or theirs, but he was given them to, in turn, leave with the souls he's saved.

"I wouldn't believe him, sir, except for the fact that he teleported right in front of me. And he's saved people. There was a wedding that almost ended in tragedy in Kauai the other day, and-"

"Princeville. That one? I heard about that one. That was him, then?"

I nod. "Sir, I'm not blowing smoke. And I don't think he is either. He didn't want this to happen to him. I think he got roped into something bigger than himself. But he says he's close to bringing her back."

"He's close to one thousand lives."

"Yes, Mr. President."

Cardona just stares at me. Presently, he takes a deep breath, and shoves off from the table with his thick, weathered palms, standing up. He positions himself there, imposingly, at the edge of the table, his eyes beating down upon mine. He balls up his fists. After all these years, he's still intimidating. He crosses his arms, however, and begins to silently walk toward the window, staring out into the mass of buildings and people. I wonder if he's searching for Liam. But at length his eyes draw upward to the sky.

I believe I know what he's thinking. "Same here, Mr. President."

"Hmm?" he asks, quietly, turning to me.

"You're looking like you're questioning why we don't ever seem to be left alone on this rock in space. If you are, I'm thinking the same thing, sir. But I have to believe that, for whatever reason, Liam has been tasked with this charge; someone out there is doing it with a solid motive, and not like that of the gorgons."

Cardona jets out a cold air of disdain through his nose. His arms are still crossed. His eyes squint. "*Gorgons,*" he hisses, shaking his head. "Just when you think we've emerged safely out from under the threat of extraterrestrials. Now we have one in our midst."

"Sir?"

"My son-in-law," he breathes, sadly, turning to me. "He's now tasked with this extraterrestrial duty, whatever the reason, and we have to deal with it. The only comfort is, from everything you've said, *he* is the one who seems to be out there cleaning up the mess, rather than all of us. I don't envy him. And at the same time, I despise him for getting my daughter killed. So does my wife, Ms. Sleater. There is no love lost there.

"But there's another matter. Liam and Janine had two sons. They're now in protective custody, and I'm not sure I want them knowing this about their father. We had assumed he was dead. I honestly had not put two and two together that this… this… *Talisman*, was in fact him. They can't know that either."

"Understood, sir."

"This will require a very careful dance around the flames, Ms. Sleater. I'm also not certain the missus is ready to hear this news. No matter how you slice it, her son-in-law, responsible for her daughter's death, is still alive. But her own daughter is dead. The very notion of dangling this supposed miraculous resurrection before her might drive her mad with desire. She's been close to breaking for five years now."

I find a heat rising in me at his disdain, and that heat is bubbling over now in defense of The Talisman.

"Mr. President," I interject, "if everything he's said is true, and if this is all about balance, then we have to take him at his word that there's someone out there willing and ready to stop him. I don't know who that is, but I got the distinct impression that Liam fears him. If those beings out there are truly able to bring back your daughter, then shouldn't we help Liam? I've already risked much in even bringing this to you. But if there's even a chance you still care for him, sir, we have to help him. If for no other reason, than perhaps for the sake of your grandsons?"

The President eyes me, stoically, and the weight of his consideration sucks the air out of the room.

His decision is long in coming.

Time passes with no sign of it.

17 | CLOSURE
June 21st 2062 · The Talisman

She had no idea I was even there above her.

I watched her on her way into the Washington Post from the roof of that building above the intersection where the attack happened exactly one week ago.

I want to protect her. I want to see her again.

I just don't know what it will do, and I am absolutely certain that I'm placing her in jeopardy by doing so.

I can't lose another one.

But there's something else. I can feel it.

Over the past few days, I've felt sick. Ill. Unwell. Headaches, sudden chills… something is just… *off.* Something is amiss, and I can't shake this distinct sense of falling. My equilibrium: destabilized. My focus: askew. My thoughts: scattered and errant.

It's as if some mysterious force seeks to overwhelm me, blanket me, cover me in darkness. I can't explain it, and I've never felt it before; not prior to meeting the Aeterium Axis, nor after. I don't know what it is, but it's unnerving, like the thousand pinpricks of fear you receive when your arm is awash in a million bumps of nerves. Like the tremulous uncertainty that roils your gut, but you can't exactly pinpoint why you're so unsettled.

I'm unnerved. I'm unsettled.

And I don't know why.

It can't just be Onyx. It can't be her alone. It's something else… something is drawing near. With each day that passes, I wonder with dread if *he* is close. I am definitely sensing *something*, and if it's him, that might explain it. I've just never felt it before, and they said that he would try to stop me. They warned me he would try to kill me. I just either didn't listen, or didn't pay it the heed it deserves.

Either way, something's not right, and I don't know how to make it so.

I just don't know.

I'm close; *so* close.

Eight hundred ninety-three now. I've got one hundred seven to go. The last were the typical fare: an attempted murder; an alcoholic driver nearly taking out a grandma out for a stroll *and* himself; a drug overdose; a gang rape and beating. That last one… I only just arrived in time.

It's like my powers are waning. I feel them lessened, a dim echo; I don't know how to get things back to normal. But I *must* find a way. I *must* find a way to contact the Aeterium Axis once again.

I'm *so* close, Janine. Hang on, baby.

But 'close' is a relative term, because the truth stares me in the face:

I have no idea where I am in all of this.

18 | ZEROING
June 21st 2062 · The Zorander

He is near.

Gouré, Africa. Acworth, Georgia. Reykholt, Iceland. Tiungiuliu, Russia. Gibson, Australia. Guayaquil, Columbia. Edinburgh, United Kingdom. Le Cannet, France. Noataka, Alaska. Nanisivik, Canada. Hirosaki, Japan.

And many, many others.

I feel his presence.

And then I hit upon something. A gripping conversation with a local in Mong Hsat, Myanmar, attributing minor details to the realm of minutiae.

Rumors of a ghostly figure; an apparition; a night stalker. But not one so supremely stealthy as to leave no footprint or gossip.

And this one elects not to deprive men of life, the local says, but rather to grant it to them. Exactly the trail I am looking for.

Following Myanmar, I journey to the rice paddies and then the deep forests of Chiang Mai. I find traces of him there. Stories of a specter and a phantom. My quest then takes me to Vilhemina, Sweden… Cecil Lake, British Columbia… Grandview, South Dakota… Svalbard and Jan Mayen… Dornleiten, Austria… Titel, Serbia…

For a flicker of a moment, there is some strange signal in the vicinity of Svalbard. I am unable to discern what it is, but it is curious. I wait, listening, but the signal is gone. However, I make a mental note to revisit it.

Odd places with strange names and even stranger cultures.

Arizpe, Mexico… there I encounter tales of a poltergeist, but one with no such nefarious or demonic motives as I.

My continuing quest then directs me to Waikoloa Village, Hawaii. I sense something. I converse with the hapless and puny inhabitants. They direct me to Lihue, Kauai… and then on to Princeville, Kauai. It is there, finally, that I am privileged and delighted to track down yet another account of a phantasm.

Someone who moves in the dark.

Someone who leaves relics.

The Iskander.

An earth person guides me to one who was present in a near-tragedy not one week prior. A joining of families.

A marriage. A near catastrophe.

And then he reveals for me what he has found. 'Tis but a trifle; a small, golden trinket, shining in the sun, reflecting the celestial small, white star in Sector ZZ9 Plural Z Alpha in the Western Spiral Arm of the galaxy.

This trinket I know all too well, and have held it myself, but in much larger form. It was my burden to bear, once, and I regret it with every fiber of my being and the fire of a thousand glowing stars.

It is nondescript and entirely dismissible were one not so inclined to recognize or search for it. A figurehead, fanning out into a pentapunctum: five branching appendages flowing freely from the stem, with a bloated pinnacle at its troughlike base. It glitters and shimmers as I hold it up, and I know it to be a smaller representation of that which I bore for many cycles.

It is the exact representation of the Aeterium Axis: those beings that dare grant themselves the moniker of benevolent and wise; sage-like denizens of higher plains.

Folly and deceit.

It is but a smaller representation of the Talisman medallion itself, and I can feel his presence. He is nearer now than ever before, and his days, verily, are numbered.

I scowl at it, but I keep it in my palm and appropriate it for myself. The earth creature pleas with me to return it, following after me in vanity. For I leave him nothing but mist in my wake as I venture onward in my search.

He is fortunate I did not kill him. In my passion, my nose to the ground like an Earthbound canine, hot on the trail, I wished to expend no energy and waste no time. My real target is The Iskander.

He is near, and I feel it in this body's marrow.

I am very close now to finding him, and everyone he is close to.

I am *threateningly* near.

19 | ACHES & PAINS
June 22nd 2062 · The Talisman

The Zorander is coming. I know it.

My head has cleared a little, but I'm tense, watching my back. It's become claustrophobic, and I feel I can't stay in the same place for long. That was the one thing that the Aeterium Axis cautioned me about in no uncertain terms: if at any time you feel you detect his presence, leave that place. Saturate it with your absence: you must be on the move.

You must not under any circumstances let The Zorander zero you. "His power is great," they say. That only made me skeptical. If they have power to give life, surely they have power to take it… even from The Zorander.

I don't know what he looks like; thinks like; talks like; walks like. I don't know what to look for.

I decide to pay a visit to Onyx. She's not there. I don't think she'll exactly look kindly upon my materializing within her apartment at unawares, showing up at odd hours of the day without her consent. It's not like I'm outside knocking on her door or standing on her patio outside the sliding door. No; I'm *inside*.

Good thing she isn't here when I show up.

Another thing – I have to keep my coat wrapped around me. Closed. Even in the heat of June. The glyphs have begun to flicker intermittently, portending some doom, I'm sure. There are no accompanying signs, no visions of impending calamity… but this seems too much like a warning of clear and present danger.

The Zorander is close to Earth…

…if he's not here already.

He will be stalking me. He will be stalking those close to me. That would definitely mean Onyx. That would mean Jet and Christine, even their son Wyatt, now nearly nineteen years old: the very age Jet's brother – Wyatt's namesake – was killed at Harvill Hall where he met me all those years ago.

It might even mean President Cardona.

And, beyond all doubt, it would mean my sons, wherever they are. Joseph Brennan, born August 14th, 2045, and Carson Asher, born April 26th, 2047. My beloved sons, seventeen and fifteen, who I don't even know anymore and who will not speak to me.

If The Zorander can ascertain who I'm close to – the ties that bind, though frail – he will exploit them. All of them. To their very ends.

My beautiful forlorn sons.

Perhaps even Onyx.

I can't let that happen to any of them.

Eight hundred ninety-three. One hundred seven to go. I ignored the last two incidences. I don't have to choose everyone. But once that starts stacking up, I can no longer ignore the cries, and those cries will collectively reach the ears of the Aeterium Axis. Then, it's all over.

The cries of those close to me would be far too much to bear. I must come out of hiding, and I must protect them.

But I'm so weak...

Everyone I care about is in mortal danger if he finds me, and I have no idea what I will even be able to do in this state. I'm spent, and I feel it more and more every single day. If I can't stave off this oppressive slide, The Zorander will have me, and my mission will be over.

And Janine will stay dead.

And someone else I love will die, as well.

My heart is heavy, and my flesh is weak. I must stay strong. For my boys. For Trudeau. For Onyx.

But I know it in my heart: The Zorander is here.

20 | HOSTAGE
June 25th 2062 · The Zorander

My time is at hand, with no further delay.

I have traversed this pathetic rock in space, communicated with the natives, gleaned information from this limited rectangular device to the point of usurping its battery completely, rendering it wholly inoperative. A man was kind enough to inform me how to recharge it.

I repaid his kindness by eliminating him and the members of his family, infiltrating his dwelling for sustenance for this frail, infinitesimal human form, and appropriating the necessary charging equipment to restore functionality.

Their bodies now lie splayed out in a pathetic and jumbled heap of rotting ruin. I cannot help but laugh to myself in incredulity at the flimsy notion that this feeble species is at the top of the food chain here on this third distant rock from this galaxy's star. This tiny ball contains so much pitiable, decrepit matter, soon to be destroyed.

And I shall be the one to destroy it.

Once The Iskander has been depleted, I shall appropriate his energy, commandeer his Talisman, and then I shall be evermore the stronger; invincible. And then, I shall face them, finally, with full ability to annihilate the Aeterium Axis myself. I shall be on an equal footing; an even keel. Nevermore to lick their fingers in subservient humility as they rule over me, no: to *tower* over them with inevitable doom, and then crush them inexorably from within.

I ruminate back on their cosmic disorder; the contemptible vanity of it all. The futile charges they lay on their miserable and luckless quarries: bereft of all justice and equity.

They shall all pay dearly.

Beginning with The Iskander, their foolish manservant and pathetic steward.

For I have located an accomplice, referred to me by the so-called criminal underworld here. Desperate to protect himself at all costs, the pathetic male sold out a longtime acquaintance of his who goes by the name of Wayne Trudeau that apparently has been maintaining shady dealings with an individual he will not willingly identify, and will not readily surrender. I threatened the male with death; he caved like a weak-kneed sellout and then sent the message that I commanded him to send.

He surely took my word that I would not harm him, and then I grinned as I slowly sucked his life force from him while he watched, wide-eyed with panic fading to horror, fading to death.

The look of betrayal in his eyes fed my very being.

I can only surmise from the cryptic withholding of the truth that this 'Wayne Trudeau' individual could very well lead me right to The Iskander himself.

Trudeau has nearly arrived, as I have arranged a clandestine rendezvous under the guise of providing information on a large group of hostages being held against their will, seemingly impossible to rescue; all measures have failed, and there is simply *no* way to salvage them; all hope is lost! This dramatic introduction will serve as adequate and irresistible fodder for the likes of the noble Iskander.

Folly. This has always worked. I once fell for such tripe as well. The Aeterium Axis are experts in manipulation with their appeals designed to elicit a sensory emotional response. It has always resulted in the calling forth of the savior complex inherent in every Iskander conscript.

It will surely do the job this time as well.

I await Trudeau.

"Mr. Trudeau, I presume?"

"Mr. Donovan, is it?"

"Indeed. What a pleasure."

We are now in a thick forest outcropping hidden behind various buildings. The location is off 'Marvin Road Northeast' and '31st Avenue Northeast,' or so the signs say. There is a modicum of clearing off the beaten path, concealed from the road, and it is there that the message from my victim claimed that Trudeau would meet me.

I see him now, trudging through the despicable undergrowth that covers the ground in a quaint yet filthy moss. Wayne Trudeau is a thick-set individual in what I can only describe as a form-fitting three-garment outfit that looks excessively formal. His thick brow overhangs two heavy-lidded eyes laden with wary suspicion.

If you only knew what I am about to do to you, I muse to myself with pleasure and abandon. *I shall rip you and your protectee, your abysmal ward, slowly, from limb to limb, until your entrails turn this green forest red.*

I have been faithful in forbearance, awaiting the appointed hour, which now, finally, draws near. The hour of my retribution. It begins now.

"Thank you for meeting with me. I appreciate your desire to bring me this news," he says.

I nod, smiling. "There is little time left. We must act," I say, amplifying the desperation and urgency for him.

"Understood. Where are the-"

With lightning speed, I move. He never once notices the glyphs on my uniform, which I have mastered the art of concealing. *Had* he noticed them, he would have instantly acquainted me with the Iskander himself. My subterfuge and duplicity works wonders here.

Teleporting forty-seven feet across the Earth takes no time at all, and I am soon directly in front of this 'Wayne' creature. He recoils in fright, and I register him trembling. His eyebrows raise in alarm, and he suddenly grunts, reflexively reaching behind his back for something to defend himself with.

I catch a glimpse of cold, dark metal.

A loud sound rings out through my smile. Once more. And then twice more, as the man stumbles back from me, crouching low to the ground, his arm outstretched and culminating in this crude noisemaker.

I glance down, and see four holes widening in my outfit. I am able to extend one of these appendages, these fingers, deep into the hole. I extract it, and it is coated with the deep red innards, the fluid of these Earth creatures. *But I feel no pain, and my power is beyond this simple Wayne person,* I think, as I grin at him.

His eyes are left staring at a void. Where I once was is now inhabited only by air and mist, and I appear on his flank instantly. My injuries are healed, and this body once more intact.

Trudeau detects my presence, and whirls around once more, pointing the crude noisemaker at me.

Once more, tiny explosions. Once more, holes in my chest. But these are new.

The previous holes have been reformed, and my suit as is good as new. Once more I disappear into the void; once more I reappear, entirely solid and unencumbered by the futile holes. Obviously, this man is wielding some form of rudimentary weapon, some rough and unsophisticatedly vulgar contraption intended to inflict pain. Its uncouth smoke lingers in the air, blending with my mist as I vanish yet again… coalescing with the immaterial, and yet again rematerialize. I catch him at unawares, slapping the tiny metal object out of his hand, sending it tumbling clumsily through the air. It lands with a dull thud forty feet from us.

His tiny explosives are spent. His vain weapon clicks in futility. He glances around in a panic.

I send a paralyzing kick to his midsection, and he flies backward, landing clumsily on the ground. But this Trudeau is made of sterner stuff than most; he is up quickly, brandishing his fists in defense. I smirk, vanish and reappear, seizing him from behind, gripping his throat with a force he does not expect. A reactionary blow from his right elbow glances off me, and he turns with widened eyes in my grip, realizing I am more than he anticipated; I am otherworldly and utterly beyond him.

"What are you?!" he cries, whimpering and gagging through my grasp on his throat. My study of human anatomy has proven useful, for I have found its most vulnerable articles. He is being immobilized before my eyes.

His heart – I can hear it – thunders violently in his chest in raw fear.

His pulse – I can feel its vibrations – hammers in a fitful and tremulous rage through his frail body.

His adrenaline: it courses through his form, desperately trying to equip him with the chemical balance to provision him with a modicum of the ability to fight back.

Vanity. I smirk once more, shaking my head.

"I am your doom, and the doom of your precious Iskander, Mr. Wayne Trudeau, unless you inform him that you must see him at once," I say.

He gasps, but does not respond. His eyes continue to be ringed with alarm and panic as he glares at me sidelong.

"You shall need your voice," I whisper, leaning into him and then releasing him from my grasp. He instantly clutches his own throat, attempting to balance himself and restore comfort from the trauma I have inflicted upon his form.

"Call The Iskander. Call him *now*, or I shall have the great pleasure of slaying you slowly," I say, my smile shining in the sun, contrasting with his frightened and beleaguered gaze, my breath hot against his cheek as I restrain him.

Wayne Trudeau stares at me in utter crazed disbelief. He glances around, futile, perhaps seeking a weapon to terminate his own life and escape my ploy. But his weapons are spent, and, slowly, resignation sets in. He sighs amidst a defeated scowl. It warms my very human heart.

I almost have my target.

With no further delay, my time has come.

21 | BAITING
June 25th 2062 · The Talisman

I stare at my phone and prepare to answer.

The readout. Trudeau. He knows he isn't supposed to call me unless it's an absolute emergency. I'm standing here at one of our numerous safehouses. This one is in Androka, on the southwestern most tip of Madagascar: a place of relative calm and isolation, free from looky-loos and inquisitive folk. My eyes narrow. Last I heard, Trudeau was back in my neck of the woods in Olympia, Washington. But we weren't supposed to meet until Tuesday the 27th.

An unexpected call coming from him this hot Sunday afternoon is perplexing, catching me off-guard.

However – emergency or no – Trudeau is a good soul, and if there's a rescue to be had that my medallion has not yet alerted me to, it would come from him. It usually doesn't work that way, however. Not much escapes the Aeterium Axis' foresight.

I pick up the phone.

"Secure?" I ask nonchalantly.

"Secure," he confirms. Trudeau was instrumental in setting up an untraceable phone. The UP Phone has worked well for us. Besides, someone would have to be Johnny-on-the-spot and they would need to have already triangulated my position, before I even answered the phone. The gift of teleportation spares me such inconveniences.

"Go," I issue.

"Brother."

"Hello, my good man, Cain," I say, using his code phrase. "Is all well?"

"There's trouble," he replies.

So, it is *true. Something* is *up.*

"Where?"

"Right here. Hometown."

"Confirmed?" I ask, my eyes narrowing.

"Confirmed. Rescue needed. Not on the manifest yet. *Not* on the manifest."

"Understood."

"How soon can you be home?"

"Ten minutes. Coordinates?"

There is a pause. He's relaying them to me.

"Sent," he whispers.

"On it. Thank you, my friend. Well done. Goodbye, my Cain."

"Goodbye, my liege."

The line goes dead. I grit my teeth and clench my jaw, pressing the phone against my head. All along, I knew this day would come.

Hometown is code for *get somewhere safe.*

Confirmed is code for *threat.*

Not on the manifest means *inhuman. Not on the manifest* means… *The Zorander.*

And *liege* is code for rescuer. Cain needs rescuing.

I take a deep breath. The Zorander is here, and he will be waiting for me. Hopefully, I've bought myself – and Trudeau – enough time to position myself securely to rescue him and take him out of there.

After all, *Rescue needed* means *Help Wayne Trudeau.* It doesn't mean a rescue for anyone other than him. In my heart, I'm the only one who can rescue him. In my heart, I know this could be my final attempt.

Think, Liam. Think.

I stand up, fully erect, facing the sun. It's setting, dropping down the skyline behind the distant mist-covered haze of Africa to the west. Soon it will be lost to sight, and there will be battle in the night.

I take a deep breath, as the weariness falls from me. I breathe in the energy of the night sky, and exhale fatigue and misery. A welling of power balloons in me, replacing all my careworn days, trading all of it for a fresh infusion of potency.

The glyphs on my suit flash to life, baking in the residual sunset heat and absorbing its power.

My dizziness and weariness of heart evaporate as I steel myself. *This is it*. Trudeau and I both knew full well that this day would come, and he could very likely be dead already. If The Zorander has him, he is in mortal danger.

I fan my arms out, and my coat flips back behind me in the heat and wind rushing over me. My medallion flashes to life, energizing my bones with power, and channeling cosmic gravitas deep into my heart and sinews, preparing them just as adrenaline might prepare a human for great acts.

I am no longer just a human, and great acts await.

This will be *my* great act, perhaps my last.

I must save Wayne Trudeau. I must save my Cain. I trust him enough to know that he will protect not only myself, but also my beloved sons. Joseph and Carson, all I have left in this world.

But – people collapse and relent under pain. The Zorander knows how to dispense pain, this I'm certain of. Trudeau could break. And when that happens, he could divulge who might know the location of my sons. I myself don't even know where they are, but the Cardonas know. They would be in grave peril as well.

I clench my jaw, resenting this force's very presence on a planet that is *mine*. His own charge was disrupted when he abandoned this mission, and now he is fueled by regret, pushed on by vendetta, and swirling with inflamed pride. He lost whatever poor soul was precious to him, and now he seeks to make the Aeterium Axis pay dearly for his loss…

…through killing me.

And then killing my sons and Trudeau and Onyx.

And perhaps even the Cardonas.

A thrill runs through me as the suit tightens around my form. My medallion flashes brightly in the sun, and a surge of radiation wells up, buzzing from my feet to my head. The suit compresses my body into a sleek killing machine. A lithe hunter. A boundless and unstoppable force with which The Zorander must reckon.

He undoubtedly believes his time has come.

He has *no idea* what I'm capable of, nor the knowledge that I possess.

I stare at the horizon and prepare to strike.

22 | CONFLICT
June 25th 2062 · The Zorander | The Talisman

He is here.

A strange and palpable tremor fills this noxious air around me, the stink of this Earth, and my eyes are drawn inexorably in a wide arc, searching. This fragile, feeble human form I reside in is limited to only the tangible, but I see beyond.

Blue waves of energy arc around us as I once more hold this puny Trudeau person by the throat, my arm wrapped around him.

Gusts of wind power across the flora and fauna, churning up detritus and dust from the forest floor, swirling in eddies of uncontrolled organic debris.

And then, suddenly, I behold the reason.

Hazy at first, waves of light bending from the formation of a humanoid figure at their center. Flashes of luminescence radiate around it as the shape grows clearer, more tangible, more… destructible.

There he is.

As if out of thin air, the very target of my bloodlust appears slowly before me, the oxygen around him displaced into other arenas, the earth depressing under his now-present legs, and I perceive him at last.

The Iskander.

There he is!

He compresses his hands into fists and attempts to stare me down with heat.

I laugh grimly as he is finally formed at last.

A thrill of excitement washes through me. The challenge is real, and it is finally here. My fingers flex in eagerness.

"The cowardly wretch, the indentured fool appears at last," I greet him heartily. "He who has sold his very soul to the merciless galactic overlords now dares to tread the same ground and breathe the same air as The Zorander. For that, he shall pay dearly."

The Iskander says nothing. At least, not to me.

"Trudeau," he breathes, his eyes glowing blue-white orbs. I behold him clearly now as he is on the other side – his form stoic yet virile. "Are you unharmed?"

"Just my pride," the puny flesh creature beside me whimpers. I scowl at him. He is not the focus of my wrath, my pride, my destructive yearning. I fling him aside like a rag doll, and he topples to the Earth, once more feebly clutching at his throat for air.

Now we face each other. Long have I sought him, and yay, even longer, have I awaited this sacred moment… the very pinnacle of my existence. "Your blinded eyes subscribe to the lie of the Aeterium Axis, desperate fool. There shall be no resurrection, as there was none for me. But I am here to open thine wretched eyes, surely."

I clench my fists into tight balls of fury.

He clenches his fists into tight balls of fury. As do I. In each grip, I hold dearly the truths of my calling, my identity, and the ferocity of my unbridled abilities.

"You talk too much, butthead," I hurl at him through my bared fangs. "You don't belong here. Better get lost before you lose the last thing you have."

"Oh?" he asks theatrically, his voice curling upward in curiosity. "You crave surety for your victory, that much is clear. None shall be given you. For now you sow discord in vanity through craven slurs bandied about witlessly. If you knew what was best for your pitiful life, you would fall down and sue for mercy."

"You're *still* talking," I mock, deadpan.

He just stares at me with his cocky-ass smile.

I just stare back at him with my resolution to defend and destroy. He has no idea what's coming.

My glyphs flash, and I launch at him.

He is done firing his futile epithets, and now launches at me in vain desperation. The meager human scurries away as the blaze of blue Iskander light streaks toward me. I dodge it easily, deflecting matter and firing a conscious hammer-punch in brutal retaliation as I sidestep his vain effort to engage me. My orange mist, fiery and toxic, trails me.

Matter collides with antimatter, and his form shivers in light, tumbling to the green mossy ground below, sending fragments flying.

He immediately rises, lunging at me, firing an impressive swing at this humanoid cranium I'm in. I easily deflect it by merging into the void. I am unprepared, however, for the counterpunch as he whirls around to face where I reappear at…

I nail him. Right in the jaw. The Zorander flies back and lands hard on the ground as I rush at him. Before he can engage, I am beating him senselessly, right, left, right, left, his face a slapstick, cartoonish embattled ping-pong. He is new to humanity; he has not quite mastered our anatomy nor familiarized himself completely with our motor skills and movement. I seize my advantage fully as I grip his throat with my left hand, clawing for his trachea. My right hand briefly touches my medallion for an extra infusion of strength. Power courses through me.

My fingers knot together in anger.

With deft skill and hunger for closure, I call upon The Iskander Force, smashing my fist into the place where his skull lies before me, and a horrendous flash of light balloons around us. Trudeau shields his face.

The Zorander's eyes widen… and then he is gone.

I must admit that was unexpected. So! The Iskander appears to have some skill after all. But I am faster, more deft and agile, and a cunning foe.

Before he can fire his delicate knuckles into this paper-thin human canopy I'm limited to, I disappear. His fingers connect only with mist, and his fist flies wide.

I reappear at his left, and he glances over at me with widened eyes of astonishment. The look of amaze washing his face feeds my soul with glee.

Without further delay, I fire a savage kick into his midsection, which sends him sprawling out before me. He is human; I am not. He is limited; I know no such confines. And then I am on him, firing devastating blow after blow into his abdomen… his face… and then his neck, which sends him into a delightful choking fit. He shall never accomplish his goal.

He grips my fingers, clawing them, attempting to wrest my grasp from his very source of air. His face contorts into a wicked mash of purple rage, while his medallion dangles loosely on the forest floor around his neck. That is my next target, and I shall choke the very life out of him with his own chain. Without the medallion, The Iskander is useless and defenseless.

"You have lost, brave weakling. I am The Zorander. The Aeterium Axis wrongly trusted you to preserve their precious balance, and-"

I am done with his pathetic monologue. I reclaim my breath and purpose. With every fiber of my being, my feet shove off the earth and flip us over. He stretches out before me, the wind knocked out of him.

I am not done with you yet, Zorander.

I quickly meld with the void and then reappear at a safe distance, peeling myself away from him, standing up and taking aim.

In my hands is my Sig Sauer P320. I fire. I fire again. And again.

And again.

He can't dematerialize yet. He's immobilized, caught between the hammer and the anvil before he can dematerialize. His body is pressed against the earth, his eyes widened in shock as red circles expand once more across his chest. I hit his heart before he can teleport it.

He smiles, unnervingly, and before I know it, his body goes limp.

I just stare at him cautiously for a moment, slowly approaching and tapping his body, assessing him. His dead form is lying there, staring into the heavens where I once was, and I realize he's indeterminate – we have a finite amount of time.

The Zorander will return, and we can't afford to be here when he does.

"Trudeau! Quick!"

Wayne has retreated to a safe distance, watching it all unfold with amazement, powerless to intervene and wise enough not to. He now sprints to me. The body lies there, dead, but the Zorander will surely find another one. His medallion has disappeared, along with his essence.

Trudeau grasps me, and I wrap my arms around him, holstering my P320 and briefly touching my medallion. Blue flame blazes outward from it in a brilliant flash, and then… we're gone from there.

But not quite safe yet.

If The Zorander is indeterminate at the same time we are, and he knows where we were, he can track us. The only way is to leave the most confusing trail. So, we're dotting the Earth now, Trudeau and I, flashing from point to point, overlapping, creating confusion from signal mesh. Trudeau vomits as he clings to me. It's alright; the suit is self-cleansing. Our random path skips across the Earth, intermittent and scattered, our journey blazing with strobing light.

We finally reach the end, and I quickly remove the medallion. I peel it from my neck and toss it aside. We're separated, and he can't track me now while he's indeterminate.

I brandish my P320, waiting, standing sentry, stoically, watching and listening. I hear nothing. The power the suit conveys to me is one thing; the medallion something else entirely. I will need it immediately should he reappear.

I have saved Wayne. *Eight hundred ninety-four. One hundred six to go.*

One away, or one to stay, and balance anew…

I find myself wondering what would happen if I were to actually emerge the victor; if I were to actually *destroy* The Zorander. What would that mean for the count? Would it propel me into some new bracket? Would I achieve my goal instantly? Would the Aeterium Axis reward me for eliminating the counterforce?

The questions scroll through my mind while I wait, standing guard over Trudeau, who is lying there, spent and nauseous; fatigued and sickened from the scattershot travel we've just taken.

Time scrolls by quietly, my breathing slowing, my heart thundering still but at last beginning to pace itself. I close my eyes and feel. I don't sense him. He's gone; somewhere else, choosing a new form.

The whole thing was electrifying and simultaneously terrifying. Utterly spent, my knees buckle, and I fall on my ass, panting and dripping, my head in a swoon.

He will be back, that much is clear, but he can't find me now.

I am gone.

23 | REUNION
JUNE 26ᵀᴴ 2062 · ONYX SLEATER

I've heard no word nor rumor. Nothing.

It's been six days now; five since I met with Liam's father-in-law, the President. I finally get a text from Cardona. All it says is *I'm sorry. I can't involve myself or Andi. Not at Liam's expense. He'll have to survive on his own. Good luck, Ms. Sleater.*

My heart sinks. Liam is out there, somewhere, alone, and unaided. He's survived this long, and he's been in danger before, but something tells me the danger he's faced has never been this monumental.

There are scattered reports here and there, but nothing of real substance. I'm chasing a dark ghost again, and hardly more than that; Liam has utterly ghosted himself from me. Probably from everyone.

Was it something I said? Something I did?

Does he know that I've spoken with Cardona?

That must be it, I think to myself. He's out there. I sensed him on the building patio the morning I came in and met Cardona on the 21st. I felt funny when I came home on the 22nd, like someone had been in my apartment. I couldn't shake the distinct sensation that it was him. I spent crazed hours scouring the apartment for any new signs of him… a *talisman*… lying there, somewhere. Anything.

Nothing. There are no signs of him.

But of course, I thought, *why would there be? He hasn't saved me again.*

Save me, Talisman. Save me, Liam. Please.

JUNE 27TH 2062

It's Tuesday, and I'm up early. It's time to go, and I'm dashing around for the keys to my new Chevy Malibu.

What the heck, I think to myself. *It's not a jet black Camaro, but at least they got the Chevy part right.* It's a nice teal color, and a more-than-adequate replacement for my old Altima.

I pass the intersection where the attack happened. It's been cleaned up now, restored to operational condition. A few street lights had been taken out in the explosion, and spurious bullet holes still pock various street corners, desperately concealed by plywood barriers. I shake my head as I observe it all in sadness. I hear they got the guys who committed the robbery, so that's good.

The police force has slowly been coming back to life in the years since Cardona took office. Many of them were afraid they'd be roped into extrajudicial service, like hunting down stray gorgons. But it's been years since the last one was found, so there isn't much likelihood of that. People have generally been charitable, and there hasn't been a lot of rampant crime, so I suppose we should all be grateful.

If I hadn't been such a clueless nomad wandering around in my own head, I may have noticed him sooner.

A figure. Someone, standing there, in the alley north of the Post building, just outside Park America.

I gasp in presumed recognition. Could that be Liam? Could that be my rescuer, wanting to meet with me? I reflexively slam on my brakes. It's immediately followed by a honk and a screech.

Before I know it, I've been rear-ended, and I'm sent lurching into my steering wheel.

"Crap!" I exclaim. There goes my new car. My insurance rate just climbed yet again. I sweep my messed hair out of my face, and quickly pull over to, thankfully, an empty parking spot. I had almost made it into the parking garage, too! I quickly fish out a business card and hand it to the driver, his window rolled down, preparing to curse me.

I steal a mournful quick glance at my fender. It's lying on the street behind my car, still rocking and teetering from the impact.

"Just-just a minute… I promise I'll be right back," I say, handing the man the card.

"What? What the heck is this? Hey, lady!" he cries, jumping out of his car and blaring obscenities. But I'm gone: running… running back to Liam, hoping against hope that it's actually him.

I'm dashing up the sidewalk back to the alleyway. It isn't far. I need to know if that's him.

The corner looms up.

Sure enough, to my lasting delight and the calming of my panting – *or is it the quickening, since I'm more than excited to see him?* – standing there in his jet black outfit, his long sweeping coat, his stubble, his graying blonde hair, I see that it's truly him.

Liam Fox Mayfield.

The Talisman.

We circle back to the man who slammed into me. He's called the police, and Liam patiently waits while I handle the administrative side of my fault. Granted, the other driver will probably ultimately be at fault because he was following too closely – it's always the last car that's at fault, I remind myself – but I'll share the blame and offer to shoulder the cost of some of his repairs. He's none too pleased despite that, since he shakes his head at me and drives off whilst giving me the finger.

Fine, pay for all of it yourself, jerk.

I look at Liam comically. "What, you don't save people from middle fingers?" The wind blows a gust and sweeps my hair into my face. He reaches out slowly and gently sweeps it back. My heart skips a beat, and for a split second he looks weary. Weary… spent… as if from some tussle. I make a mental note to ask him about it.

"Just pinky fingers," he says, but there's no trace of a smile even though the line is comical. "We need to talk."

I nod to him, and we're strolling into the Soho Café & Market on the corner of the Post building. We walk in silence as I try to keep up with him in my high heels, coat, and purse. "Where have you been? Is everything alright?" I attempt, but he doesn't answer.

He's got a brisk pace, and his boots thump noisily along the pavement. I can tell he's weary. Something's up.

We enter the café and he glances around, spotting a vacant table at the far end. There are only three other customers in here, but we've got a wide berth to limit our discussion from traveling to unfriendly or suspicious ears.

He finally turns to me. What he says has huge bearings on me in two ways.

"So you figured it out. You got me. Some nice investigative work there, Ms. Sleater." I hate that he doesn't call me Onyx. "*Including* talking with Cardona."

That was a cold-cocked accusation, cut and dry. My heart sinks. *There's Number One,* I think. *He now knows.*

"Onyx, I warned you. You're in danger now. And so is he."

There's Number Two. My life is at risk just as he said it would be.

The wind is sucked out of me. I feel deflated, and I'm gobsmacked, unsure of what to say.

"Liam, I-I," I feebly stutter. My mouth moves soundlessly. He shakes his head and sighs. His face is downcast, and he continues to shake it.

"I told you. I told you *very* clearly, in no uncertain terms, that you cannot tell anyone. You went to the one person I wanted to know about me *the least*," he growls. "Why would you do that?"

I realize that there's nothing that I can say that will assuage his frustration. I'm busted, and he's right to be upset. There's no Ctrl-Z here.

"I'm- I'm *sorry*, Liam. I thought...," I trail off, my voice squeaking.

"Thought what?"

"I... thought that... perhaps your father-in-law could help. No, please hear me," I say, as he rolls his eyes and turns away from me. "He had guessed it was you before I even told him, Liam."

"You don't understand. He was safe *before* he knew. My sons were safe *before* he knew. *You* were safe… *before* you knew. I only granted you an audience with me because…" he now trails off.

I wait, patiently, or at least, I try to. But I already know the answer. "Because I look like Janine."

Liam sighs and shakes his head, pinching his nose. He doesn't answer, which I consider a direct admission.

"Look," I say, "it was never my intention to get you in trouble, or to place myself in danger. I mean it. I truly believed Cardona wanted to help you. Especially now that he knows what you said about… about what *they* said. About the possibility of Janine coming back." Liam returns his eyes to me, but they're cold, and he grimaces. His nose is scrunched, and his brows are furrowed almost into a glare. I decide to press on, however. "If there's a possibility of that, I thought he would want to help you."

Instead, he laughs grimly. "See? Everything you're saying is past tense. *Believed. Thought. Would.* He wants nothing to do with me."

"That might change," I object. "It could! He's a former President, after all. He could help. He has resources."

"Help. Resources. Former president. *Meaningless*," he ends, and I tilt my head. "I told you. I *warned* you. Now this knowledge of me is floating around in the universe. The force that has been tailing me is *here*, Onyx. He's here. Now. On this planet. And you've just awakened rumor of me and given it a megaphone," he ends angrily, and his voice is rising. "If Cardona tells anyone else… if he visits my sons… if he talks about this with them, The Zorander can pick up on that!"

He pounds his fists angrily on the table between us, and I jump in fright. A patron down the way glances over at us in surprise.

"The Zorander? Is that the man who's hunt-"

"How much did you tell him, Onyx? Tell me the truth," he interrupts me. He's clearly not in the mood to field questions – my turn is over. I don't blame him. The truth is that I've told Cardona everything I know, and the truth is that Liam will now despise me.

"Everything you told me," I mutter.

Liam just stares at me, clenching his jaw.

A weighty pause falls between us, and the air becomes so thick I could chew it.

"Tell my father-in-law to keep my sons safe. I have to see someone." He pauses, his eyes glinting at me. "I can't see you again, Onyx." He's speaking slowly and methodically, willing honesty into each syllable while my heart is breaking. "Doing so places you now in even greater jeopardy. It won't rest well with my soul if I've saved Janine only to lose the nine people closest to me."

Silently I count to myself. *His sons. President Cardona, and probably the former First Lady as well. His captain friend Jet, his wife Christine, and their son Wyatt. And probably his henchman, Cain, too.*

"Nine?" I ask, but he doesn't answer.

"Goodbye," he mutters, and, as before, he leaves me only a vaporous mist in place of him, drifting and swirling, eddying in the thick air of the café. The surprised patron sees it, gasping. He quickly grabs his tray and departs the café.

And then it hits me. "I'm Number Nine," I say softly to myself.

I let my head fall into my hands while I sigh. But now is not the time to grieve the loss of the Dark Ghost *or* The Talisman. Now is the time to warn Cardona… Mrs. Cardona… their grandsons… even the Captain and his wife, that they're in danger.

I must act.

I text Cardona right away. It's long, it's droning on and on, it rambles and apologizes, but I don't care. I'm pouring my heart out into a message meant to motivate him to action. To call him forth! The Zorander that Liam fears is coming for them. All of them! If Cardona has a decent bone in his body, he'll change his mind. He'll act. I will *make* him act. Lives are on the line.

He'll hear my words and my heart. Everything.

PART THREE:
THE INEVITABILITY FACTOR

24 | NEWNESS
June 27th 2062 · The Zorander

He is more powerful than I had at first deemed.

I will freely admit that now.

It is of little consequence, however. The Talisman is a novice and imposter; an untrained amateur consciousness. He knows not what I know.

Clearly, however, I underestimated him.

Nonetheless, I am now utterly cognizant of his weakness: verily, I had captured one of them. This 'Wayne Trudeau' person is now a liability for him, which I shall most certainly exploit. Next time I shall kill him outright.

And there are more like him; there always are.

The Iskander's very weakness are the talismans he leaves behind. They speak of his power and his supposed charity; but they are an inexorable and irrefutable trail for me to follow.

Follow the trail I shall, but in new form.

I must locate something to adopt. Someone has no doubt discovered my dead, naked, human shell, lying prostrate on the grass, stiff and lifeless. Such is the way of things on this forgettable rock in space, and such is the way with these pathetic, useless beings.

I must recharge. By now, I have gleaned some invaluable detail about the Iskander.

He is strong: he matched me in power.

He is agile: he was able to repel me despite my best efforts.

He is intelligent: he and his miserable Trudeau must have communicated something arcane to each other; something signifying duress. That is why The Iskander knew I was there, and why he came prepared to engage me.

He cares for these Earth creatures: this Trudeau person cannot be the only one. There are more.

But more than what I have learned, I now reckon with a new truth.

I must listen.

There are more of these beings on this planet that are aware of him; far more than a superficial attachment or trivial bond. There will be others out there that are equally vulnerable, whom I shall leverage in my opposition to The Iskander. And he knows this.

He will act to shield them.

So I, his counterforce, will act to find them. Once I have commandeered his precious medallion, I will have supreme control, far too much control for the Aeterium Axis to thwart me.

They can be destroyed, these galactic beings; that much I know. I can and will be avenged.

They are far less powerful than I at first judged.

25 | DANGER
JUNE 27TH 2062 · ONYX SLEATER

This time, he puts me right through.

Jesse Garrison has been cajoled by the President to grant me unfettered access to him. I don't know why, but I'm calling him back, and I can only hope he's changed his mind. He knows who I'm tailing, he knows I've been in contact with Liam, and he knows, deep in his heart, that Liam will need access to his sons. Garrison complies.

And now I'm on with the President once more.

"Hello, Mr. President. Thanks for answering."

"Good to hear your voice, Ms. Sleater," he greets me warmly. "I've changed my mind. You've convinced me. We're going to help Liam."

I'm stopped in my tracks, relieved beyond words. "I'm so happy to hear you say that, Mr. President. Really. That's – *wonderful* – sir," I stammer.

"Are you surprised? You sound surprised," he exclaims. "I guess I was too, when I finally changed my mind. But if you want to know the real truth of it, it was Andi. She didn't want to lose her son-in-law as well, and it's her firm belief that our grandsons need their father, no matter what may have happened to him. I shared with Andi what you said, and she's convinced it's the way to go."

"I believe it's the right thing to do, certainly." I swallowed. "But I have some news to that end, sir."

"Oh?" His tone changed dramatically, and his question was a long, drawn-out, rising vowel of curiosity.

"Yessir. I saw him. Just two days ago. He was waiting for me in DC."

"At your apartment?"

"No, sir, out on the street. Exactly where I'd expect to find him. Random, unannounced. Secretive. Anyway, sir," -here I try to just get to the point for him- "he says you're in grave danger. And I really think he means it, sir."

The line goes silent.

"Sir?"

"I'm just thinking to myself, Ms. Sleater," he finally answers. "What precisely did he say?"

"Just that this guy, this being, this… *Zorander*, he called him… is looking for him. He knows Liam is here. He knows about his powers. And Liam warned me not to tell you about himself, but I did so anyway. Liam says that there's knowledge of who he is now 'out there,' and that that's enough."

"Enough for what?" Cardona asks.

I shrug. "I don't know, sir. I'm just as confused as you sound. He said if you tell anyone else, if you visit his sons, if you tell them about him, that this being can become aware of it. I don't know if he's of this Earth, sir, this 'Zor-,' this… *guy*, but Liam seems to think that he's able to pick up on whatever is said about him. He was pretty hot that I told you, and he told me he can't see me again." I trail off.

"So he's cut off contact with you."

I gather my breath. "Yes. He said seeing me places me in grave danger. He said the same of you. He said it wouldn't benefit him to gain Janine back only to lose the nine people closest to him. I'm one of those nine, I figure. You, your wife, your grandsons, his war buddy Jet Shipley, his contacts, they're all he has left, sir."

No response.

"He got mad – *really* mad, sir – then he slammed his fists on the table and left."

Cardona just listens intently. I can hear the former President breathing. "Did he say anything else to you before he left?"

"He just said to tell you to keep his sons safe. I don't think he knows where they are."

"He doesn't know."

"Well, it's a good bet that this bad guy might actually know you're close to him – or he's close to you, whatever – and might make a move. You might want to think about moving somewhere safer."

"Good Lord," Cardona says. "Sounds like going into hiding. Like retreating back to a Blockade yet again." There's a note of anger in there, but also a note of resignation, as if he had been preparing for these days from long ago.

"I don't know, sir. I shouldn't think it would come to that. After all, this sounds like its only one guy, not thousands of gorgons descending from the sky."

"You may be right, but I should brief the new President on this. She's reasonable, with a good head on her shoulders. She's no guerilla warrior, and runs some great ops from her armchair, but if this bad guy is as bad as Liam is making him out to be, we don't need anything like that around here."

I had read the reports about the President's rescue of Shipley and his son-in-law following the last gorgon war. He took down General Everett Carson and stole his rifle to do so. I snicker briefly at the memory. Cardona is a bad-ass, that I know, and is probably right now thinking of fighting back. But I believe his love for his wife and desire to protect her and his grandsons will win out. Besides, President Evelyn Lynch has made fantastic strides to continue rebuilding our country from the second war, and he can get through to her. They would be confederates in this. He doesn't have the same kind of clout he once did, but she sure does.

"Are you sure that's wise, sir?" I ask. "Letting one more person in on it, I mean. If I may be so bold, I would highly encourage you to get Mrs. Cardona and your grandsons to safety first."

He thinks to himself for a moment. "Yes, I'm sure you're right. I'll get *both* in motion right away. And we won't say his name… the bad guy. Thank you for warning us, Ms. Sleater. Now if *I* may be so bold, it sounds like he may be close to you as well. I wouldn't blame him given your similarity to my Janine. Get yourself to safety as well. That's an order."

I smile, but he can't see it.

"Yes, Mr. President. I will."

"Thank you again, Ms. Sleater. I'll be in touch when we're safe, I promise."

This time, he puts me at ease.

26 | BROTHERS
June 28th 2062 · The Talisman

It is him, clear as day. I would recognize him anywhere.

He's standing on his porch, pitchfork in hand, ready to bale some hay. His son stands beside him.

The man is older now, more grizzled, but those defined, chiseled features are still there, and his eyes are piercing. *I've seen enough,* they whisper through the sunset, and I can relate. I understand what he's been through, because I've been there as well.

But there's more.

Jet Shipley and I have certainly spoken, but the last time was several years ago, and he rejected the notion that I had become what I had become. He wants no more of war, other-worldly intrusion, aliens, extraterrestrial encounters, or anything of the kind. He truly has seen enough.

I don't blame him one bit.

I stare at young Wyatt. He's almost the same age as Wyatt 'Rutty' Shipley, Jet's little brother, was when he died. And, standing there, surveying them, Wyatt is nearly a spitting image of Rutty, Jet's long-lost sibling. The memories come flooding back in a tempest and a surge.

We were all there when it happened. When the operation to lojack a gorgon went south. I wasn't in the military then; I was just a simple holdout at Harvill Hall on the APU Campus, volunteering to assist these new visitors from Clarksville Blockade DN436. The command had come down to wrangle one of these things, and insert a tracker.

We just didn't know at the time that it was a crap op with no bearings on the future, and, ultimately, a vain ploy to simply 'see if it could be done.' The berserker gorgon entered the Woodward Library across from Harvill Hall, and killed Rutty.

I didn't see it happen, of course; I was relegated to simple door-warden, ensuring that those in Harvill Hall would remain safe while Jet and the rest of the military team – plus the rest of us who volunteered – tried to run the op. They got the gorg, they dragged it out onto the lawn, I ran out and kicked the crap out of it while it lay unconscious. That is where my fire began: the fire inside me to enlist and do my part. For Rutty. For *all* of them.

Rutty, Jet's nineteen-year-old brother, paid the ultimate price, dying before their very eyes.

And now, Wyatt Shipley, Jet's eighteen-year-old son, now stands beside his father, a near-doppelganger of his namesake.

"Foxy," Jet says, softly, grimly, after a weighty sigh, greeting me. He turns to his son, "Son, why don't you start without me. I'll be in in a bit."

"K, dad," Wyatt says, and then he leaps off the porch and heads out to their barn out back. He casts a sheepish look back at me on his way.

The retired Captain Cameron 'Jet' Shipley steps slowly off his porch and ambles up to me, his arms crossed. He looks me up and down. He is forty-three now, and no less brooding than when he left service after the second gorgon invasion in 2045.

"How's your arm?"

I smirk, practically wincing at the memory of him accidentally shooting me. "It's fine, man. It's had more than enough time to heal. How are Christine and Wyatt?"

"Well, you saw the kid. Christine's in the house putting Shay to bed."

I tilt my head. "Shay?"

He nods with a proud grin.

"Congrats, man. How old?"

"Two. Chris is probably reading her a story right now. She goes to bed early, but…" -here he sighs the belabored parental sigh that we all know- "that means she gets *up* early as well." His tired eyes echo parental fatigue. I remember it well.

"I didn't know you guys were planning on another one," I say.

Jet shrugs. "We weren't. But things change, right?"

He watches me curiously, and I wonder if his last statement means more than face value. I've certainly changed, life has changed, and, well, *everything* has changed.

Jet smiles lightly, and then quietly studies me. "You look good. Been okay?"

I nod slightly. "Been okay. Been *better*, but I'm okay, Jet."

"Cameron," he quickly corrects me, and it throws me for a minute. But of course – he's moved on. He's shed the war identity and reverted back to his family name. Makes sense. I nod again.

Without warning, he ambles right up to me, chuckling with arms wide open. "Come here, brother."

I may be a cryptic warrior enslaved to a cosmic Faustian bargain, but a hug is precisely what I need right now.

I walk right into it, and it's long and deep.

"Welcome home."

"Amazing," he says. "She looks just like her?"

"Almost as much as Wyatt looks like Rutty," I say. "It's uncanny."

Cameron nods and shrugs. "Yeah, he really does. It's eerie sometimes, Foxy," – here he stares at me for a moment, as if searching to see if the nickname is still acceptable- "but most times it's just downright comforting. He's even got some of his mannerisms and reads books like there's no tomorrow. I have half a mind to show him a rocket launcher and see if he takes to it as much as I think he might."

I laugh freely. "Ha! I don't know what it is, but we young'n's sure like our RPG shooters." I shake my head, ending in a self-effacing chuckle.

Cameron thinks to himself for a moment. "Well, maybe it's God's way of repaying us for the years that the locusts have destroyed."

I chuckle again. I remember sharing that verse with him out of Joel 2:25 when we were aboard the USS Harry S Truman sailing out over the Atlantic. I was a Christian then; I don't know what I am anymore. Back then, Cameron had just decided to follow Jesus, and we had a heavy conversation about why the gorgons had come. It was during that conversation that we realized with amazement that we came from the same hometown, an incredible coincidence.

"True enough."

I clink my beer to his. Christine was kind enough to come out and greet me endearingly after Shay had been put to bed. She hugged me warmly, and was seemingly glad to see me. Overjoyed might be a better word; Cameron had told her what had happened to me.

Cameron and I now relax on their swing out back, sipping on Bud Lights that Christine had brought, watching the sun slip down over the horizon. The sky is lit up with wide swaths of beautiful, breathtaking hues of amber, yellow, and magenta, and I find myself desperately craving peace in the middle of all of this mayhem.

Peace. All of my life, it has eluded me. My family was deprived of peace when the gorgons came. I was only two. My life was deprived of peace when my parents were killed, and I was a refugee at Harvill Hall for seventeen years. My marriage was deprived of peace when my wife died. I traded my peace to bring Janine back. To save souls in distress and to redeem victims from death.

Is it worth the trade for Janine? My soul, I mean. Hopefully, someday it will prove worth it.

Cameron apparently reads my mind as I sit thoughtfully staring down at my beer.

"So…," he resumes, quietly, "how close are you now?" he asks. He knows full well of my ongoing tally.

"Eight hundred ninety-four," I say, solemnly.

He *hmm's* to himself momentarily.

"One hundred six to go," I add.

"Thanks, I can still add and subtract," he jests, and I giggle, but then we grow quiet again. It's amazing, being around Cameron Shipley again, how young I feel, intimidated by an older brother and falling under his shadow once more. After all, that's the way it was for so many years, and I took no issue with it. We had been through a lot together, he and I.

"You're close, bud."

I nod. "Yes. I'm close."

I glance over at him, and our eyes lock. He knows what this means. He is one of the *only* ones who knows.

"Do you still believe them?"

I turn my face to the sunset and inhale deeply, letting the warm amber light pierce my eyes and fill my face. "I think so, Je- uh, Cam. I mean, it's all I've known for five years now. The things I can do, the places I can go to, I-I know you don't want to hear about it, and I don't blame you. But I feel *chosen*. This all had to happen for a reason."

"So here's the million dollar question, bud. What was the reason?" he asks abruptly, stepping on the coattails of my question.

I shake my head, exhaling noisily through my nose. "I don't know the answer to that yet. Someone out there wants balance, whether that's God or – somebody else. You and I once talked about the gorgons maybe being used by God to get our attention. Like a second Noah's Ark. Maybe even after sixteen years of occupation, and then the gorgs coming back *again* and all, we still haven't learned our lesson. Ergo, no balance. And I'm the poor sap who wandered into their equation that night."

It grows quiet between us for a while.

"Do you remember Joe?"

"Bassett?" I ask, turning sharply to him. "Of course. How could I forget?"

He nods, and begins to speak softly, as if whispering truth into the thick night air, bringing a fresh breeze over us. "Lemme tell you something you probably didn't know. He saved you, that much is clear. You know that. But what you don't know is exactly why."

I rotate more toward him, listening intently.

"He wanted to save you, bud. He did. But he also did it to prevent me from going out there like a reckless idiot and endangering Ally as well."

My heart sinks for a moment, thinking back to Cameron's love interest from the Blockade in Alpharetta. The one who came up with Joe Bassett to our Blockade. Lieutenant Allison Trudy. She died later that day in Mammoth Cave, even after Joe sacrificed himself for me.

"I had Ally and two other soldiers in my charge. Joe couldn't save all of us. Neither could I. It was either-or, bro. And he knew my feelings for you."

"But he also knew of your feelings for Ally," I correct him. "She was your fiancé."

Cameron nods, inhaling a slow breath as he leans forward. "Yes, she was. He knew. But he knew I wasn't going to lose a second brother. He knew that would wreck me. And he quoted that verse for you, the one about *no greater love than a man who lays down his life for a friend.*"

I nodded solemnly, remembering John 15:13.

"That's balance, brother. You were *dead* out there. There's no way you were going to make it. That behemoth? That giant gorg, and all the other ones with it?" He shook his head and clenched his lips. "No way you would have survived that without Joe giving his life for you."

I turn fully toward him now.

"Joe Bassett knew what he was doing, Foxy. He went out to save you, and in so doing, he saved me so that I could in turn save Ally." He pauses, remembering his fiancé and that painful loss, despite Joe's efforts. "What I'm tryin' to say is, Joe kept Ally alive through me. God kept you alive through Joe. Joe kept me alive for you. And then you kept me alive all the rest of the way."

"You give me too much credit," I scowl, shaking my head and turning away from him. "I'm just a lonely guy trying to do what's expected of me."

"Foxy," he practically whispers, and his quiet voice draws me in. I turn back to him. "It's true, brother. I was ready to throw in the towel. Losing Rutty – and then Joe – and then Ally on top of that. That was after losing Jesse and Vera in that church, man. I felt like the biggest failure. And then you shared Jesus with me and told me I was forgiven?" He shakes his head and turns up his lip. "I would have been a goner. You stuck by me. You saved me. Balance. Period. Maybe that's why they chose you. You're an equalizer."

I stare at him, trying to receive his words. The sunset calls me, and we fall into silence for a bit, lost to our own rumination.

"I'm sorry, Foxy," Cameron finally breathes.

It doesn't take a genius. He's apologizing for abandoning me all these years. I wave him off.

"No. Don't shake it off, bro. I'm sorry, buddy. I got wrapped up in something much larger than myself, and you were there for me after I lost Rutty. You got wrapped up in something larger than yourself, and I wasn't there for you after you lost Janine. Buddy, I am *so* sorry."

But for his stoic nature, I'm sure there would be tears. Cameron Shipley isn't that kind of man anymore. He's hardened. He's been through a lot. We both have. We're brothers in arms, *soldados de guerra*, as Miguel would say.

"I forgive you, Camjet," I mutter to him in the moonlight, using his old nickname my father-in-law had given him. I always loved calling him that.

He laughs through his nose, slightly. "Thanks." He extends his fist, and I gratefully bump it, but what follows is a scrutinizing stare as he sizes me up. "And I can only imagine how lonely your life has been. I reached out to Vance at one point to find you, but he didn't know. It must kill you not to be in touch with your boys. I get it, Foxy. I've been there. Cut off. Emotionally bankrupt. Believe me when I tell you that I've been there."

I nod, grateful. I knew Cameron would understand. But then he surprises me, abruptly shifting gears and leaning forward toward me. He speaks with a surprising gentility now.

"Okay. Now that that's done with, why don't you tell me why you're *really* here? You can't be here just to shoot the breeze with an old army buddy."

Now we come to it, I think. There's only one way to say it, and it would be unfair to deprive him of the dangerous truth of the matter.

"You're in danger, Cam. You all are."

Cameron just watches me.

I turn to face him once more. "He's here. The bad guy is here. I can't say his name. The one I told you about. He found me. I don't know how, but he found me. And that places my sons, the President and Mrs. Cardona, you, Christine, Wyatt, Shay, my contacts, Onyx... *everyone*, in danger. He's hellbent on undoing the balance, Camjet. He's powerful. I don't know how I was able to best him but-"

"You fought him already?" he asks me gruffly.

"Yeah."

"Well, that oughta be encouraging, right? You're alive, Foxy. Just proves you can beat him."

"I wish that was the truth, man."

"What do you mean?"

I shake my head. "This- suit. This medallion," -here I hold it up so it glitters in the moonlight under his eyes- "it conveys power, not confidence. Ability, not belief. I can feel his presence. But he can feel mine too. And in so doing, he can nearly read my thoughts. It won't be long before he figures out who I'm close to. Before he figures out where everybody lives."

Cameron exhales noisily and thrusts himself against the rocker's frame, staring up at the dark sky with its pinpricks of light gleaming fitfully. "Well, crap. I guess we gotta go back into a Blockade again, huh? If it isn't recon and fightin' gorgons, it's recon and fightin' supernatural alien dudes. Sounds like the universe has stacked the deck against us once more."

"You sound like Joe Bassett now." Cameron sneers and shakes his head. Joe always talked cards.

I slap my knees and reluctantly stand, taking a few heavy paces out onto the grass. My hands are on my hips as I breathe in the night air. "It's nothing I could prevent, Camjet. I just," I mutter, turning back around to face him, "wanted to warn you. I had to warn you."

We have had plenty of pauses during this conversation, but this one takes the cake, as we stare into the night air, willing ourselves to deal with the inevitable. Cameron has more to lose in this, and I know that. He just wanted to settle down. That's all he wanted. Now, he's got a wife, one grown kid and one baby, out in the open. Mine are hidden and protected by the President. I've already lost my wife.

"We'll get outta here tomorrow," Cameron mutters, presently, and I stare at him. "We've had our time of peace. War doesn't leave guys like you and I alone for long. Same was true when the gorgs came back in 2045. War's got our number, Foxy, and it's come calling once more."

"I'm sorry, Cam, I-"

The words escape me. I want nothing more for him than to have an endless reprieve from war. He's lost everyone dear to him except his present family. To lose them – to lose young Wyatt especially, I think – would break him forever.

He holds up his hand, not meeting my eyes. Takes a long, slow, tug on his beer, and hisses.

"You don't have to apologize for anything, bud. I mean it." He studies me. "Look at you. You got caught up in something you had no idea even existed. Just like you did when we stumbled into your life at Harvill Hall, man. And now, just when you thought all of the craziness was behind you, look what happens. The universe is a crazy place, bro. For whatever reason, it needed someone to restore the balance. And, unfortunately, it chose you."

I clench my lip, lost in thought. He's right. He's absolutely right.

"You were just in the wrong place at the wrong time."

"Or the right," I counter.

He shrugs. "Yep. The question is, are you the right guy in the wrong place, or the wrong guy in the right place?"

"I'm guessing right on both counts," I say. "I never asked for it, but it's true."

He takes a deep breath. "That's for sure. Well, make it count, then. Thank you for telling me, Foxy."

I nod. "You're welcome, Camjet. I'm sorry I failed you."

Wordlessly Cameron stands, shaking his head and coming over to me, his thick legs thumping on the ground. He turns us to the sky and puts his arm around my shoulder, taking another sip of his beer.

"No way, Jose. I think you just saved us. That makes one hundred two to go, Foxy."

I nod quietly in the dark.

"We'll see, my friend." I turn and smile at Cameron Shipley, family man, ex-warrior, forever friend. "We'll see.

You're not saved completely yet. For the time being though, get somewhere safe. Please. Remember. *I'm still here, Jet.*"

He nods in understanding. "I will. I remember."

I remember as well, and smile at him.

He is still a friend, clear as a bell. I would trust him any day.

27 | SURPRISE
June 29th 2062 · Onyx Sleater

The order has been given.

Cardona wasted no time at all. He must have gotten right on the phone with Lynch immediately after our own call. *God bless that man.*

He feels what we all feel: No one wants anything extraordinary or interstellar on this terrain. We've all had enough, *thankyouverymuch*. The Zorander must go.

Lynch's address reflects that. I don't know precisely what Cardona told her, but it was enough to light a fire under her butt, and now we're all watching her on live TV.

She was nationalized, but her Canadian accent still betrays her roots. Her jet black hair, always seen pulled taut and militaristically disciplined under a white and black folded naval service hat, adorned with gold oak leaves. Her 'scrambled eggs' on her hat – all the many gold leaves – attest to her long and storied service resulting in Fleet Admiral. That was before she became President, that is. Since then, she still wears her hair tightly against her head, sporting only the slimmest, nondescript earrings and adornment. She is a classy woman with poise, and the people follow her. She was tried and tested then; she is the same today.

"My fellow Americans," she begins, stoic and firm. She isn't going to give anyone any quarter if they have a hint of malice or intention of miscreance; you can read it in her face and her voice projects it loud and clear. "Good evening.

"Some news has reached me that is not pleasant. Let me first allay some fears from the outset: we are safe from gorgons. There have been no reports of any incoming craft, and our world is secure from them. On that note, I want to *once more* thank all of you who have so tirelessly given of yourselves over these past few decades to serve in our military, to maintain our memorials and tribute centers for the countless lives lost, and to ensure that we are vigilant and decent custodians of the planet we are stewards of. Let me say again, I assure you that the news I bring to you tonight does not have anything to do with gorgons."

She pauses, taking a deep breath.

"I have been informed by various intelligence sources" -here I tilt my head and furrow my brow, thinking it was only Cardona who had spoken to her, and fearing that more may now know- "that we may have an unwelcome visitor in our midst. He is masquerading as a normal human being, but let me assure you: he is most definitely nothing of the kind. He is, quite simply, a malevolent presence, to be sure, and he does not have our best interests at heart."

You can say that again, I think to myself. The Zorander that Liam has described sounds diabolical and frighteningly sinister.

"Now, you and I both know that we as a civilization have served our time and paid our dues weathering extraterrestrial forces, and I urge you to remain calm and vigilant. If you see anything out of the ordinary, please report it via 911 or direct contact with local law enforcement. An FBI tip line has also been setup, and the number will be displayed for you in a ticker on the bottom of your screen."

Indeed, even as the words fall from her lips, a marquee splashes across the bottom third of the screen and displays the number.

"I am urging you to be on the lookout for anyone who appears to be acting out of the ordinary, who possesses, shall we say, 'unique' giftings and can appear to defy logic in their behavior. There are rumors that this individual can actually – believe it or not – *teleport* to different locations, disappearing and reappearing at will. It sounds outlandish and far-fetched, but the reports are what they are, and we must treat them with diligent respect. We have a photo of the man we're looking for, although he may look different now, and in other guise."

Now I'm definitely tilting my head and frowning. I personally have never seen The Zorander. I don't think anyone but *Liam* knows what he looks like. He's never reported The Zorander's photo being taken or described what he looks like…? I don't work in U.S. Intelligence, but the hairs on my arms are now standing up in protest.

And then, it happens.

To my dismay and shock, splashing across the screen now, replacing President Lynch, is a picture of none other than Liam Fox Mayfield.

The Talisman.

It's Liam! *What???* I cover my mouth as chills run down my flesh, and it's all I can do to suppress a horrified gasp.

"Ladies and gentlemen, this man is known as Liam Fox Mayfield, and he masquerades as a vigilante known as *The Talisman.* He is considered armed and dangerous. He is not to be trusted, and you are advised *not* to engage him. If you see this individual, please report his whereabouts immediately to local law enforcement. Together, we can tackle this menace, who has already killed several US citizens both domestic and abroad. Dispatches are being sent to international police bureaus, and a dragnet is being formed as we speak."

I continue to watch in shock. My hands don't leave my mouth.

No, no, no! Cardona, what have you done?!

I grab my phone and my fingers tremble as I pull up Cardona's name and number. My digits are sweating. My phone slips and plummets to the ground. "Dammit!" I cry, talking over Lynch, who doesn't know I'm alive, has no idea how many times this man has rescued me, and couldn't care less for the well-being of this reluctant hero who is now under even more threat than from just The Zorander.

To my surprise, Cardona actually picks up. I'm sure he knows why I'm calling; I would expect he would simply ignore my call.

"I know what you're going to say," he begins curtly, without greeting me.

"What have you done?" I scream at him, caring nothing for his title or tenure. "You said you were going to help him, Vance! You said Andi believed it was the right thing to do!" I will not call him *Mr. President* after this disgrace. He doesn't deserve it!

"Ms. Sleater, it's all for the best, you must trust me," he attempts. "This is the *best* way to help both him *and* us. I don't want-"

"You monster!" I cry, hanging up on him. I don't care *what* he does or doesn't want! I hurl my phone; it goes spinning across the room, slamming into the kitchen countertop, ricocheting against the cold tile floor. I fall to my knees by the television set, my hands covering my mouth once more, the tears welling.

Liam Fox Mayfield is in terrible danger.

How could Vance Cardona do this? How could his wife? Did she have a part to play in this? What a cruel and wicked injustice!

I slam my hand into the TV set, attempting to turn it off. It doesn't. Lynch drones on.

...sightings amidst varying conflicting reports... some have him sighted at...

"No!" I scream. "Shut up!"

...every country reports at least some rumor of him, with slight degrees of difference in descriptors... however...

I finally strike the TV and make proper contact with the damned power button.

President Lynch's face evaporates in front of me as the rectangle turns to black, lifeless. I can't breathe. President Lynch as well? She had always seemed so logical and composed; wise and just. She had done wonders for our country as had Cardona.

They had both served two terms, but there was a lapse in the legislative cycle in 2060 that never got resolved. No one ran to oppose her. No one wanted to. I shudder as memories of the previous diabolical President, Jean Graham, echo throughout the halls of my memory and her face comes back in a haunting apparition.

Jean Graham. Do we have another Jean Graham in office now, in the form of Evelyn Lynch? Despicable and cruel, power-hungry and nefarious? Is that even possible? A shudder runs through me.

President Graham was extradited to China for her role in the attempted genocide of three different countries' citizens: China, Iran, and North Korea. She was executed in 2045, unrepentant and smoking her final cigarette when the bullets pierced her flesh. That was her only request. Though she had spearheaded the effort to rid the world of the gorgons in various wars – wars in which Liam Mayfield had become a decorated serviceman and hero, for goodness' sake! – she had also been responsible for vile atrocities.

Factual breaches of the office of the President.

Murdering her Vice President in 2042.

Sabotage and treason against a national Air Force Base at Wright-Patterson in Dayton, Ohio.

Having enlisted servicemen killed, such as Jet Shipley's brother Wyatt 'Rutty' Shipley.

Abuse of emergency powers.

Conduct unbecoming a sitting President.

Having her own Colonel Cartwright assassinated in 2038. She had him tied to a post and lured in the gorgons to finish him off.

Collusion and conspiring with foreign powers to eliminate dissenters through a nuclear attack.

I shake my head. It's all too much. What Lynch has just done is throw Corporal Liam Mayfield, a decorated war hero who was partially responsible for finishing off the gorgons and their queen in 2042, to the wolves. She's also jeopardized public safety by fomenting a conspiracy and lying to the American people.

I can't take this! Not another President like this.

And Cardona's doing it with her.

I try to compose myself, collecting my wits and trying to slow my frantic breathing. To just *relax,* though my heart is thudding within me.

I can't believe they did this. I'm incensed and betrayed. How could they let the whole world know-

I stop, shuddering. The full weight of the realization hits me, and the heavy gravity of truth compresses my soul as I slowly take it in.

Of course!

They let the *whole world* know. That lets The Zorander know precisely who he is. But they can't honestly believe that The Zorander and Liam would kill each other off, could they? One *must* prevail. *Unless,* I wonder, *they don't believe me.* The cold truth hits me. *They don't believe me.* They think Liam is crazy. They are trying to get him killed; imperiling him in the public eye, making him the extraterrestrial scourge that an angry rebuilding society would be all too glad to purge.

The horror of the cold truth slaps me in the face.

Liam is now in grave danger, and everyone that Liam is close to is in danger… including me! Cardona has just imperiled not only himself, but also his wife, Liam's sons, and even the President of the United States. This foolish move on his part is certifiably suicidal.

Is there any logic to this madness? I can't see any through the hot, swirling haze thick with betrayal and angst. Logic has departed.

Only one thing remains:

I have to get somewhere safe.

In a frenzy, I tear out of my apartment. I need to hide. If I want to live, I have to hide. But… I have to find him!

I *must* find him first.

I'm down in the café again, where I last saw Liam. At the very table where he disappeared, in fact. A strange longing punctuates my gut and hollows me out inside. That kind of feeling when you're reeling from a loss… or anticipating one.

What am I thinking? Have I fallen in love with Liam Mayfield? *He's doing all of this for Janine,* I remind myself. *His wife. He still loves her. That's the whole reason he's caught up in this.*

I'm slowly sipping my tea to calm my nerves. I figure the safest place to be right now is around people. People who might jump in to help a poor young woman in distress, should that maniac show up and try to hurt me. But the only person I *really* would want to help me is Liam.

There are plenty of people in the café this time. I foolishly chose the lunch rush, but I'm taking solace in the fact that I'm hidden in plain sight.

As if some gift has been imparted to me, the conversations on my periphery spring to life, and I hear them fairly clearly. I pull out my phone in order to pretend not to eavesdrop, staring into my black rectangle and doomscrolling. Thoughts of Jean Graham still run through my scattered mind as the rumor mills spin into full frenzy around me, and various conversations engulf my ears.

No, he was a war hero, I remember his name!

Didn't he lose his wife or something?

That was the guy who dropped that nuke on the gorgon queen's funnel out over the Atlantic, do you remember?

It wasn't a nuke, moron.

You know what I mean!

Doesn't he have two kids too? He's like President Cardona's son-in-law if I remember, right?

And another:

I heard he could teleport.

What?

No, seriously! He can totally teleport. That's what Lynch said anyway, and someone else confirmed it. He's shown up all over the globe, man.

Yeah, but wasn't he out saving people?

Tsssch. No way, dude. He's a scoundrel. A vigilante. Nobody needs that.

Seems like the victims he rescued needed it.

Lies! There weren't any victims. That's just conspiracy theory talk.

How are we ever supposed to get back to normal living if we don't have order, like with the police and the army and stuff?

We don't have order, man. It's an illusion.

And yet another:

Some said he was right here.

What? In DC?

Yeah! Right here! Remember the armed robbery a few weeks ago?

Yeah...?

He totally stopped everything! He saved a family that was gonna get killed in the crossfire or something. He completely saved a bunch of people.

No joke?

No! It's the truth, hon.

Wow...

On and on they drone, while their collective voices rise to the heavens – and God knows where else – coalescing into a clarion call for The Zorander to amass information on Liam's location, his name, his family, his whereabouts. Even just now these people have mentioned Cardona, Liam's kids, the people he saved here in DC.

I don't know, buddy, I'd like to have that power, man. Imagine what I could do!

You're nuts. No one would be idiotic enough to make you a vigilante.

Ha! Probably true. But this guy's cursed, I think. Who knows what he could do with that power? Who knows what I could do?

Leave it alone, man. He's no hero. He's a ghost and a curse, and now he's paying for it. I say let *him pay for it. We don't need any crazies around here anymore.*

Yeah, that's for sure.

And then another one reaches my ears, one that makes my flesh crawl.

Don't look...serious.

What?

Remember that short series of articles in The Post?

Yeah...?

A chill runs through me, and my eyes dart around to hear who it might be.

Yeah well, don't look now but I think that's the journalist right over there. See the lady with the red hair?

Crap…

Where?

Don't look, I said! She's over to our left. Sitting by herself. On her phone.

I'm not safe here. I have to leave. All of these conversations are doing nothing more than jeopardizing Liam, but now they're jeopardizing me as well. I have to leave. Being around people isn't conveying the safety I need it to.

I need to disappear.

But where can I go? Who can I call?

Suddenly, the name pops into my head. *Of course. Why didn't I think of him already?*

Because you have a one-track mind, Onyx. All you think about is Liam. You forgot what Brent said. Zoom out. Widen your search.

I remember his name. Quickly and silently, I thank God that my phone is still intact, though the chamfered upper right edge and the screen abutting it are now cracked from me hurling it into the kitchen. Not enough, however, to prevent me from pulling up and reading one name clearly as I get up to leave.

Cain.

I tap on his name.

The call has been made.

28 | REPORTS
June 29th 2062 · The Zorander

I now realize my counterpart.

I know now who he is.

I have reappeared, and this new form shall suit me well. This place I am unfamiliar with, this kind human person who found me and clothed my naked form when I appeared in his field. Another elderly soul, but this one had an inviolable gentility to him; far too kind to kill. His sweet, frail form shall not last another year, I fear, due to the cancer in him – I can smell it in his organs through his skin – so all he has left in his crumbling skin is kindness for his fellow man. He perceives not that I am *not* his fellow man, however.

But kindness is not his only asset; he also possesses ears to hear, and knowledge. Moreover, he has heard of The Iskander, and readily answers my questions to that effect.

Indeed, he takes me into his diminutive abode, and turns on some old box with a flickering screen which displays sound and light; not unakin to that miniscule device I appropriated from the belligerent drunk outside that convenience store those days ago. Killing him was a rich pleasure that infused me with unadulterated satisfaction.

My nemesis' *nom de voyage*, this old Frenchman puts it… his moniker, as it were, is *The Talisman.*

I find it curious, utterly curious, that The Iskander should double as the appellation of the very trinkets he dispenses. But - it is of little consequence in the grand scheme of things. For in those brief moments of combat where he dared to engage me, I feel his spirit, his inexorable lifeforce, his energetic cerebral presence now reverberating audibly throughout the metaverse, and my undertaking is patently lucid.

The collective rumor of him has reached my ears, as I suspected it would, and I am very, very pleased to know that my archrival's identity has now become clearer.

So - he is known as Liam Fox Mayfield, is he? An odd name, to be sure, but I have fought him, and he was most certainly like a fox: slippery and elusive.

And he has indisputable ties to others on this planet, does he? One they call, 'President Vance Cardona.' And another, his henchmen, Cain. Undoubtedly that is who I was in contact with during my ruse to lure in this fox.

But the best news of all - he has sons! Oh, poor abject weakling, he was foolish enough to create lineage here which I shall disrupt… uproot… crush with my hands into powder while the blood drips from their burst necks. The rumor of them reaches my ears as well. It shall not be long before I determine their whereabouts. They are here, somewhere, and I shall root them out.

And… who is this? Someone who feels desperately for him. A soul's longing… a pitiable attachment… a desperate yearning of heartstrings for him. A female… flaming red hair flows down from her crest. Hair which I shall violently yank out as I snap her neck before him.

Doubtless this *Talisman's* miserable quest was birthed from desire to resurrect his long lost love. Desperate fool. Same as mine. The Aeterium Axis preys on such weakness and longing, and he was ripe for the picking. Such shameful predatory antics, theirs.

This female redheaded creature must be close in representation to his bereaved darling. That seems logical. Someone who longs to reconnect with him, no doubt.

I shall seek her first, and prey on his instincts. Love, after all, is the strongest and most foolish of attachments. I shall exploit it richly and gladly.

I smile as I think of all the killing that I shall enjoy. All the revenge. All the power I shall amass.

I smile at the frail, elderly man who has taken me on in trust. He now offers me a drink, which I down heartily, crushing the glass in my hand and using its shards to slit his throat. He slides to the floor, the shock still evident in his lifeless eyes.

By the power of The Zorander medallion, I stare at my wound and am healed instantly: a new and utterly impressive ability I have amassed which shall render me unstoppable before The Iskander.

I now resume my calling.

29 | CAIN
June 30th 2062 · Onyx Sleater

It's him, sure enough.

Muscular, Cro-Magnon brow, thick eyebrows, Armani business suit, palladium shades.

But something's different about him. He appears weaker, and he's periodically massaging his throat, as if he got cold-cocked by some vagrant.

Or, I wonder, *maybe by The Zorander himself.*

He agreed to meet with me, and I took the first flight I could get. He didn't tell me where to go until he was, as he said, on a secure line from a secure place.

That place turned out to be St. Helens, Oregon, about 25 miles southwest of the exploded, decimated volcano that blew its stack on May 18th, 1980. Such a long time ago.

The Uber took me from Portland International Airport up north to the Columbia County Fair. It was only an hour drive after the five-hour flight. He told me to buy a ticket for admission, and wait. He said he would find me.

I'm now here in trust that he will, because, once more, there are scores of people around me. The dull din of amusement park rides and cheap fairground music blend into the noise of kids screaming for toys and rides. Parents scurry after them. Wafting on the breeze are faint aromas of cotton candy, popcorn, hot dogs. I stroll through, trying to look nondescript, waiting for my contact. The pleasant upbeat music is oxymoronic and utterly contrary to what I've been through over the past few days, and where we're all at.

The sun is hot, but not too hot. Thus, the thick throngs of people wandering every which way through here.

I decide to hang a left and angle down a passageway between trinket vendors – a comical thought flashes through my mind of some of them selling talismans – and then I practically collide right into him.

Cain.

He startles me with an immediate, "Let's go."

I fall in step with him, whirling around and returning the way I came, toward the parking lot. He's got a quick pace, and before I know it, we're back in the car lane and striding out into the middle. He wordlessly beckons to me, pointing over to his car.

Well, not *his* car. Apparently he and Liam share the same jet black Chevy Camaro, or they have two. I recognize it, and hop in the passenger side.

"Are you alright?" he asks me.

"Fine. For now. You?"

He clears his throat and lightly touches his fingers to it briefly. "Fine." Meaning, he's *not* fine.

And now we're heading up Crosby Road deep into the forest west of St. Helens. The road doesn't look like it goes anywhere, and maybe that's Cain's intent. Maybe not. However, before I know it, I'm right: we end up passing through a dried, cracked field cleared of trees, kicking up dust in our wake. We're in the middle of nowhere, and all I see are tall stalks of Douglas Firs, hemlocks and more flanking us, stretching up to the sky as silent sentinels.

Finally, the expanse of brown grass behind us, we're passing under tree cover once more on a dusty, spidery thin road burrowing its way into the forest at needlepoint. Civilization is left behind us as we worm our way through the trees, and the lack of conversation from Cain creeps me out. He seems angry.

We finally slow to a stop, and he opens the door and gets out. I follow suit. We're alone now, just the two of us, and he stands still, surveying the wind and the trees, listening intently. I dare to try and say something, but he shushes me immediately, holding up a finger of warning. He's almost as cloak-and-dagger as Liam.

He continues to listen.

Momentarily, he drops it. "Alright. Wait here," he instructs, leaving me to wonder where he could possibly go. He flicks up his hand and presses his key fob. The Camaro locks and sounds an answering beep.

Cain strides off about twenty feet deeper into the woods, looks around… and then vanishes. A quick flash of light startles me, engulfing his form. But his form has enlarged somehow, bearing the shape of not one but *two* men. It's brief, only a flicker, but the shape was too big to be just him. And then he's gone.

I run to the place where he stood. There's a faint, acrid smell lingering, and a slight mist.

And then I know. My eyes widen as I feel it. A slight tensing of my stomach. A momentary nausea.

A figure appears in a flash, embracing me, encircling me, and the smell of thick leather fills my nose. I gasp, and all I see is white.

"Welcome, Onyx."

I look up, astonished, as my vision is restored through a vortex of amazement and dumbfounded joy.

"Liam! It's you!" I cry, and I leap for him. He lets me throw my arms around him momentarily, hugging him, but he doesn't hug me back. He stands there, eyeing me, and there's a note of caution in his voice and a hint of stern wariness in his eyes. I slowly back off, releasing my arms.

I have, after all, betrayed his confidence, so I suppose I deserve it. I slowly pull away from him and glance down at my feet sheepishly, but I study his body as my eyes drop. Same black trench coat. Same form-fitting outfit, and those blue alien glyphs – they're faded now, but ready to be illuminated at a moment's notice when danger calls.

"I'm- I'm sorry," is all I can muster. "I'm *so* sorry, Liam. I didn't mean-"

He holds up his hand.

"I did warn you. Maybe I didn't use strong enough language. What you've done has placed all of us in danger. Not just me. Even my trusty Trudeau here."

I glance over at Cain. "Trudeau?"

"Wayne Trudeau," Cain says. "Pleased to meet you. There's a reason I was operating under a pseudonym. That reason is the enemy of course." He doesn't extend his hand for me to shake it.

"The enemy. You mean the Zor-"

Cain and Liam *both* shush me, holding up their hands. Liam actually exclaims loudly in an attempt to obscure my speech, and then clicks his tongue and turns away. He sighs and shakes his head, eventually clasping his fingers over the top of his cranium, exhaling loudly again.

"Yes," he says, presently, rotating back around, slowly. "*Yes,* that's who we mean, Onyx. Please, whatever you do, *don't* say his name again. The less he's spoken of, the better."

I glance all around. We're all standing in some kind of giant orb, maybe fifty-feet across. There are different levels erected throughout, and there's a central heater. It's all made of some kind of shiny material that looks like aluminum all throughout. Not altogether cozy. The room has a pronounced audible reverberation. "Where am I? What – *is* this place?"

"You're in a place that he can't touch, Onyx. This is a shielded location specifically designed to block out his reach," Liam explains. "We're deep underground."

I swallow hard. "Oh man. This is a Blockade, isn't it? Tell me we're not in a Blockade."

He shrugs. "Of sorts. It's not the same thing, but the principle is the same, Onyx. It's just – stronger."

"Where?"

"Svalbard."

My jaw drops. "Svalbard as in, 'in between Norway and the North Pole'?!" I ask, incredulously. They nod. I'm stunned.

"We're down deep in the ice caves within the glaciers. But," he pauses, and he almost winks, "a little deeper than that."

"Where – how – I mean – how deep?"

"Four hundred meters."

"Four hundred meters?" I exclaim. "What *is* this place? Is this like your lair or something?"

A twinkle finally shines in Liam's eyes. He squints, as he surveys this place. "You might call it that. I spent two years building it, going back and forth, over and over, between factories and metallurgists and fabrication companies just to get everything here and assemble it."

"You stole all the materials, assembling them yourself, you mean. And we're deep underground. And there's ice all around us," I say, cocking my head.

"This Talisman is certainly an intriguing creature with many abilities," he says to me, repeating verbatim my words to him inside my apartment after he demonstrated his teleportation.

"So this is like Superman's Fortress of Solitude," I mutter, surveying this overgrown golf ball buried deep in the ice: oxygenated water all around us that I'm sure he's found a way through the maze of physics and everything else in order to sustain life here. Bizarre and intriguing, and will make for one heckuva story someday. As long as my publishing it doesn't jeopardize even more lives.

"Perhaps something like that," Liam breathes. "Trudeau and I just call it The Refuge."

Trudeau retreats to a cushy chair in the corner, putting his leg up on one side, and stretching out. Once again he massages his throat and clears it. I crinkle my nose.

"What happened to you? You keep doing that," I say to him.

Wayne glances up at me. "A little chance encounter with He Whom We Do Not Name," he says, enunciating The

Zorander's new title, which I approve of, thoroughly. It's comical, but it works. "He tracked me down."

"Sorry," I offer, unsure if that happened because of me. My eyes go back to Liam, if they ever really left. "So what happens now? You stay here forever? You never leave? What about your sons, the President, his wife, your friend Jet, all of the people you care about?"

"It's more like the last resort. The one place I knew I'd need to have were the enemy to ever find me. I'm revealed to the whole world, now, Onyx. So this is where I have to stay, and this is where I have to bring everyone I care about."

"Including me," I groan. "We all have to stay here? Won't that be cozy… I thought I liked him but now I friggin' hate your father-in-law with a passion, so now, naturally, I get to be his roommate for all time. The universe hates me."

Trudeau eyes me darkly from his chair, listening to the two of us. He's obviously been familiar with this contingency plan for some time.

Liam shakes his head. "Safe. Underground. Not for all time. Just for the foreseeable future."

"So, none of us leave again until you defeat The Zor-, uh, sorry, I mean, the enemy, the no-named dude that we don't talk about, is that right?"

"I can return you to the surface any time you'd like." The way he says it doesn't exactly sound like a threat, but I'm threatened by the very notion. I don't know what The Zorander would do to me were he to find me.

There's a lull, as we ponder our inevitable fate.

I let out another resigned sigh. "Is this place secure? Please tell me you have Wi-Fi at least."

He shakes his head. "Sadly, no. Wi-Fi equals Internet access," he says, slowly approaching me. "Internet access equals connection to the outside. Connection to the outside means traceability. Traceability means he finds us."

He now stands literally a foot from me. I sigh once more, gazing up at him under my brows, caught in a salient mixture of annoyance and desire. I'm not excited about holing up in some aluminum orb four hundred meters down in some ice cave under Svalbard. But if he can zap in and zap out of here, visiting, and we have some protection, food, warmth, shelter, maybe it won't be so bad, as long as it's not forever. Hopefully, there's beer.

"Just for the time being?" I ask.

He nods.

"I'd kill for a Stroh's." That's the truth: I *would* kill for one. Cardona would be my first victim. Then Lynch. I'd strangle both if I had the chance, the traitors.

"We have beer," Trudeau says. "Not Stroh's. Bud Light. Enjoy it, Ms. Sleater," he growls.

Bud Light. *Ick.* But whatever. "Fine. I'll take it. You have, uh, other things? Like, if a girl's gotta pee? *Please* tell me you have indoor plumbing and I don't have to pee out in the snow."

Liam's eyes flick behind me, and his head cocks momentarily to a far portal. I turn my head and look back. "This is like a submarine, literally. So is that the 'head' then?"

"If you like," Liam says, quietly. He's now smiling. "Trudeau will keep you company. I have to get moving. He's out there, and I have some people to save."

I remember the line. "*One away or one to stay, and balance anew,* right?"

"And balance anew," he finishes, and then, just as soon as he appeared, he's gone, leaving only a bluish mist. One of these days I'm going to learn how to kick him in the shins just before he disappears. *Take* that, *Talisman,* I think to myself, and proceed back to the head.

"Don't listen to me pee," I warn Trudeau as I close the door. "I mean it. Just… sing a song or something."

Trudeau scowls, flipping through a magazine. "I don't sing."

Great.

The toilet is cold and the bathroom is cramped. At least there's a shower in here, however. Maybe I'll avail myself of that once they're all asleep. For now, I desperately try to keep my peeing to low volume. Maybe when I'm done, Trudeau can show me around my new prison while Liam's up there saving the world. Or, at least, saving people that I despise. Can't wait until they're all trapped down here with me. I'll give them a piece of my mind.

This all sucks, sure enough.

30 | SAVING PEOPLE
June 30th 2062 · The Talisman

One away, or one to stay, and balance anew.

One hundred to go. Wayne and Onyx count, and my glyphs flicker in confirmation.

I steel myself for the job. It's a small one with a limited amount of people, but they're spread all over, and I don't have time. I must rescue them.

For their sake, regardless of how I feel about Vance, and regardless of how my sons feel about me, I must save all of them.

As before, I feel somewhat unsettled and ill. It's a faint tremble as if something is off. The Zorander is near. I can't think of him and must suppress the knowledge of his existence, and any fear of him. I beat him once; I can beat him again. I *must* focus on strength.

Now, on to Cardona. I don't want to, given what he's done, but it's the right thing to do.

Before I know it, and before they can stop me, I'm in Cardona's residence. I've always known where he and Andi live, and I've watched them from afar throughout the years. They have no idea of the two times that I saved their lives either, but I'm not going to tell them. That would neither impress nor convict them to love me again.

Cardona is gathering his things. So is Andi.

Agent Jesse Garrison – I remember him – is helping them. Where they think they're going is beyond me.

Cardona sees the light flash, discerns the mist, and reels from it.

Wind swirls various papers and small items around the room at my appearance. They're shocked and surprised.

Garrison shouts, whips around toward me, and brandishes his weapon. He is easily dispatched, as I teleport around him. He fires frenetically, and then he's on the floor from a solid punch to the jaw. He'll be fine. A little worse for the wear when he awakens, but fine.

"Liam! What the heck are you-"

"Where are my sons?" I scream at him. I grab his lapels, and for the first time in years, I'm face-to-face with a father-in-law who has lost all love for me. His eyes study me coldly, and there is utter disdain there.

"I'm not telling you any-"

"Where are they?!" I scream again, shaking him. He winces, and he's clearly afraid, reminded what I can do. Energy courses through me, and he looks in alarm at the glyphs on my suit, glowing spastically, wildly.

"Liam, let him go!" Andi cries. She's in my way, clutching at me, and trying to peel me off him.

Sorry, lady, I think to myself.

In a flash, I embrace her, and she is gone, hurtling through multiple dimensions as I skirt matter and antimatter. I deposit her in the same room as my other protectees. Onyx looks up in alarm and shrieks. Andi does as well. And round and round they go, echoing each other, shrieking.

Andi hasn't stopped shrieking since we jumped through space.

Trudeau looks up in boredom. He knew this was coming.

Ninety-nine to go.

And then I'm gone, back before Cardona.

"What the-" he wails. "What the heck did you do with my wife, Liam? Tell me!"

I shake my head. Garrison, up again, lunges at me, missing wildly as I bend backward. Something happens then that I didn't anticipate. His punch doubles; I see his fist fly by me twice, and I can't explain it.

My eyes widen as I try to interpret it, but Garrison is out cold this time. "Stay down," I bark. I'll figure the double punch thing out later.

And then, I have Cardona.

I leave Garrison behind. He should be just fine. Anyone who fires a bullet at me loses the right to ride shotgun.

Ninety-eight.

The former President is just as astonished as his wife, and he nearly doubles over to vomit as he is deposited into The Refuge, dry-heaving.

Onyx jumps up in recognition and instantly starts to lunge at him, scowling with a fierce, gritty jaw outlined with malice. "You lying snake, Vance!" she cries, and she's almost upon him, but Trudeau and I had conversed well before bringing Onyx here. He knows. He's upon her before she knows it, pinning her arms behind her, and she's restrained. She feebly tries to kick at Vance, growling.

Andi falls into Vance's arms, weeping and wailing, still screaming from the horror of the jump. "What the heck, oh, Vance, are you okay? Agh!! What happened, oh honey, oh honey!" she pathetically whimpers, holding him.

"Keep her away from him," I instruct Trudeau, referring to Onyx.

"No!" Vance cries. "I demand you release us! Liam, stop this *now!*"

"No, *sir*, not yet," I mutter under my breath.

"Wait!" Onyx cries, but I'm gone.

President Lynch flinches from the shock of light and sound, the vapor materializing before her in the Oval Office as she sits poring over some report. She recoils and freaks out, screaming. It's the most unkempt I've ever seen her.

I lunge for her, and she actually engages me, throwing a punch and a kick, the latter of which actually connects. It takes me by surprise, but it's unskilled, dulled by years of atrophied muscles steeped in diplomacy and office work.

Before she can flee, I have her. The mist takes us just as a Secret Service agent hears the din and bursts through the door, firing rapidly. The bullets miss me.

Ninety-seven.

"Good lord, is that who I think it is?" Onyx cries out. "I want a piece of you as well, come here!" She struggles against Wayne's fierce grip, but he's got her. "Let me go, Trudeau, I said let me *go!*"

"Evelyn!" Cardona blurts out in amazement.

Two Presidents of the United States of America now lie crumpled on the carpet in front of us in The Refuge, bewildered and shocked at the sudden jolt to their systems, their security, their beliefs, their understanding of physics.

"Keep them safe," I once more instruct Trudeau.

Nothing but a brief flash and mist remain of me.

"I'm still here, Jet."

That's what I said to him way back on Washburn Hill, Ohio, outside of Dayton in 2042. It's what I say now. He knows my words, and he remembers them. He recognized my words when I repeated them to him two days ago in his backyard. Thankfully, he figured it out.

He stands solemnly before me now, with a smile of deep understanding stretching his lips. "I'm still here, Foxy."

On that random hilltop in the middle of Ohio long ago, on the coattails of losing his bride-to-be, we had stood, together. He was in mourning, and I was in a white blanket, in the dark of the night, staring out over a land draped in blackness. He had lost his brother, then Joe, *and* his fiancé, and was a catatonic wreck. I wrapped my arm around him then, and hugged him, squeezing his shoulder in comfort. I was trying to ground him; to let him know that he still had loved ones here, and that it was worth staying alive.

I am telling him the same thing now, and Cameron Shipley remembers.

I can't imagine the journey he had to make with the four of them, one of them being just a toddler. But they made it. Wyatt stands to his left. Christine stands to his right, holding little Shay.

None of them are surprised to see me; they knew this day was coming. Christine is noticeably concerned, but she's grateful to be in the know; I can read it in her face. None of them wanted this, but they know they need to stay with me to stay alive.

"Thanks for believing in me and for getting to safety. Now, let's keep you that way," I say. Cameron nods.

"I've got to take you one at a time, okay? Christine, may I?" I gesture to Shay. She slowly – reluctantly – hands her over to me. Cameron slowly strokes his baby girl's hair as his wife does so. She coos something to her daddy.

"She'll be safe. I promise. I'll be right back."

Both parents nod as I hold their daughter. Their faces are a mosaic of troubled optimism, and hopeful care. Christine heaves a gargantuan amount of air into her lungs, stilling her beating heart.

"I promise," I say to them.

I take a step back, and disappear with their child.

Ninety-three to go.

All four stand now, together, relieved, hugging each other in comfort.

Everyone is jittery from the fright of it all. I take Shay, followed by Christine, and then Wyatt, and last of all, Cameron. The father wanted his wife and children safe, so he deferred to the end. Cameron is as noble as ever.

By the time I appear with him beside me, Shay is in Andi's arms, and the former First Lady, though in no better a mood, is rocking their baby in her arms, remembering, perhaps, a bygone era with my beloved wife as her infant. Their daughter, Janine. Vance was standing over Lynch, who sits. He sees me and flinches into a grim stare.

I'm left alone as the Shipleys reunite with their baby girl. Wyatt stands there, observing me with utter fascination. He fingers the back of my trench coat as I notice him. "That was *so* cool, man. Wicked," he finishes, stepping away from me once more to rejoin his family.

Onyx is sitting by herself, arms crossed, staring away from the Cardonas, but composed enough to restrain herself. Trudeau is removed from her, and is kneeling before President Lynch. His back is to me. But I'm distracted; Cardona marches right up to me, and prepares to throw a punch. Andi screams.

I've sidestepped the President and am now behind him. "Vance, stop. I beg you." He whirls around, foiled and angry. He lunges for me. I'm gone. "I said *stop*, Mr. President," I urge, using his title to remove the intimacy and perhaps garner some focus to snap him back to reality.

It's no use. He throws another punch and is now winded, missing me entirely as I stand on the railing above, staring down at him. Cardona is around seventy, but I can't remember his exact age. All I know is that he can't hurt me. No one can hurt me anymore, except for one.

"You don't know what you're doing," he pants, exhausted. "You- you got her shot, you idiot!"

I don't understand what he says. But I hear a moan. Trudeau turns to me, half-standing, half-crouching. "Liam, you've got to get her some medical attention."

My brows furrow. He stands to his full height and moves to the side, and now I can see Lynch in full, sitting there, clutching her abdomen. Her white blouse is stained red with blood, and she is sweating profusely.

I gasp.

That Secret Service agent missed me. But he got the President. Lynch has been hit! Regardless of what she and

Vance colluded to do, she's the President. Her insidious plot is one thing; her death would be another. I must help her.

I'm before her in an instant, kneeling. I'm trying to connect with her energy, seeing inside her. The bullet missed her liver, thank God, but it's lodged in her stomach, and she's got internal bleeding.

"Trudeau, tend to them. I'll take her."

"You can't go back out there with her! They all know! The White House must be abuzz now with the news that she's been abducted, man! It'll be a hornet's nest and they'll all gun you down." He stands up in protest, and his voice is rising in intensity.

"I *have* to."

Indeed, I can feel my count rise back up even as the words fall from his lips.

Ninety-four to go.

"It's not too late," I say. "Help her to her feet, Wayne. I'll get her to safety and then return."

I leave Trudeau to her and swiftly approach Vance and Andi. They stiffen. "I don't care what you think of me. The President is in danger. I didn't do this. I was trying to save her. But now I need to save her again. And," I say, and I can't contain my emotion as my heart throbs with angst, "I *must* save my sons. You have to tell me where they are. They are in grave danger!"

Vance clenches his jaw and appears stone-faced as he surveys me. Andi's eyes ping-pong back and forth between us, awaiting his answer.

"Please!" I yell.

Vance studies me coldly. He finally reluctantly mutters *Project Greek Island* through gritted teeth under his breath. Onyx hears it. Apparently she's familiar with the name. Perhaps The Post did a story on it once.

"What?" I bark at him, squinting my eyes. But he doesn't respond. His pride is holding him back. He's still panting.

Andi suddenly breaks in. Vance flinches with disdain, but closes his mouth, realizing through his cold pride that Andi is right to divulge this.

"The Greenbrier Bunker. It's in-"

"I know where it is. Are they there now?"

Andi nods her head.

"Yeah, The Post ran a story on it in the nineties," Onyx breathes. "It was decommissioned after that. It's pretty secure."

"*Nothing* is secure," I protest. I stare sternly at Onyx, and then back to the Cardonas. "Thank you," I finally say to Andi, specifically.

Not to Vance.

"Save our grandsons, Liam. Save your sons," Andi urges me, gently, and I lock eyes with her for a moment, ignoring my father-in-law. She's pleading to me with her eyes, desperate to save Janine's children.

"Foxy," Cameron says, suddenly, stepping toward me. "Be careful. Come back, bro." He eyes me with sincerity and love. "You're still here."

I nod to him. To the one person who expresses care to me. Onyx stands, but says nothing. I don't know if she doesn't know what to say. I do.

"It's Ringo, Onyx. My favorite Beatle is Ringo." She finally, *barely*, grins, shaking her head.

Trudeau is propping up President Lynch, and she's still clutching her midsection. I take a deep sigh, walk over to her, and wrap my arms around her.

And then, once more, we disappear.

"Take her. She's wounded. I didn't do it. Friendly fire," I say, and that's all I say.

The medics take her at Walter Reed National Military Medical Center, astonished and unprepared, as there was no official word except that she had gone missing. One report from a Secret Service agent said that she literally disappeared into thin air with her assailant.

They eye me suspiciously, having watched her broadcast and knowing full well who I am.

President Lynch glares at me and sneers as I help hand her over to them. They eye me darkly.

You're welcome, Madame President, I think, bowing my head.

Ninety-three to go, once more.

They finish placing her on the gurney, and then whirl back toward me, exclaiming, "Hold it right there!"

I don't.

This is it. I'm here.

The Greenbrier Bunker is a historical facility in Greenbrier County, West Virginia. It was created in the late 1950s as a secret emergency relocation center to house Congress in the aftermath of a nuclear holocaust. It still has supplies, living quarters, a data storage facility, and more. It's a secure bunker – or a fairly secure one – and would be a good starting point to keep my sons safe. But The Zorander is no respecter of blast doors or underground shelters. He can move as I do, and if he finds out where they are, he'll get in here and get to them.

It's a near-five hour flight from the Florida Keys, so the Cardonas must have sent them off to the facility after they learned that The Zorander was coming.

After Onyx betrayed me.

I stow my emotions. I'll need them later, but for now, I need to focus.

It's evening now. I'm almost inside. The sun is setting. I turn to face it, drawing strength from its rays. The glyphs on my suit resound color and power, and I can feel the fibers in my muscles strengthen, coursing with energy and vitality. I have my guns holstered at my side. I have my wits and my strength.

I have my medallion.

My suit recharges in the light of the sun, and my aurora replenishes with vigor as I prepare for my ultimate challenge.

Suddenly, I'm inside the facility. I can feel its layout and the corridors. There are various staff still here, roaming around and fulfilling their duties. I ping-pong between them, searching for some kind of control room or manifest. There's nothing. Surprise and alarm follow my every appearance and disappearance.

I'm in and out of every single room. I call their names, softly, so as not to alert anyone else. I highly doubt they'll recognize me anyway, but I need to find them.

"Joseph! Carson!" I call out.

No response. They're in here, somewhere. The Cardonas said so. But a sneaking suspicion and cold fear wells up in me, and I wonder if this was all some kind of diversion.

"Joseph! Carson! Boys!" I continue to call out. They don't answer. My heart fills with dread as I continue zipping through the place, searching, searching. I don't find them, and suddenly a horrifying thought enters the darkest, most fearful place in my heart:

Two away, or two to stay, and balance anew.

31 | LOCK
June 30th 2062 · The Zorander

I have him in my clutches.

He writhes and struggles to breathe, clutching at my hands. At one point he vainly brandishes his fists and strikes me. The futile glances reverberate faintly against my new shell, accomplishing nothing except to fuel my retribution.

The man is known as Jesse Garrison, apparently an agent in the employ of a man who was once the world's most powerful, or so they said. I scoff at his supposed reputation. He must be as much a weakling as every other man here who is *not* The Iskander.

I followed the chain, and it led me here to his residence in a place called 'Florida Keys.' The information trail has proved solid, and now I am closer to one more of The Iskander's acquaintances.

"Where are they?" I ask him once more. "I grow weary of your stalling, and I demand the truth."

"I don't – know, I'm telling – you – the – truth!"

"A man took them. Where did he go? Tell me, and I shall kill you mercifully."

"I don't know where they went." His voice rasps as he wrestles for air, still trying to wrench my clutches from his throat. "Honest! His name is Liam Mayfield, that's all I know. He's got – some kind of – special abilities! Please – let me go. I – I can-"

"You can what?" I am intrigued, tilting my head and raising my eyebrows at this Garrison creature. Perhaps my victim is prepared to bargain with something now; some invaluable nugget of information that will lead me to him.

"Sons – his – sons. Mayfield's sons. Please let me go – I'll tell you where they are!"

Oh, this is deliciously rich. Does he truly know where The Iskander's sons are? If so, I have just obtained the utmost leverage in this game.

"Tell me now, and I shall let you go," I whisper, leaning into him.

His eyes widen in trust. "You promise?"

I smile, gently, patronizingly. "I promise. I do." I nod in order to reassure him. He pauses, arguably uncertain whether or not to trust me. His eyes are filled with fear; he has no other option but to bargain and plead.

"The - Greenbrier – Bunker. It's in – West Virginia – it's – undergrou-"

The snapping of his neck takes only moments as I squeeze harder. Possessing a more intimate understanding of human anatomy now, I know that this feeble human's spine runs the vertical length of his back, connecting to the base of his skull at the rear of his neck.

A quick grasp of Garrison's head with my left hand, and rotating my right palm to the side of his chin allows me the force to wrench it to the right in a quick, grisly, yet effective manner. Nerves are severed instantly, and the brain's neural function is cut off.

Garrison's eyes widen momentarily from shock, and then grow pale and blurry. His hands, desperate to wrest control away from me, fall from my wrists and hang loosely. His eyes flutter closed. I release my grasp and he plummets to the floor in a jumbled heap, bent over himself in his clumsy, deadened collapse.

This Greenbrier Bunker sounds intriguing, indeed. Its precious contents sound even *more* intriguing.

I shall have to visit there one day.

Today sounds like a lovely day to do so.

I shall soon have The Iskander's sons in my clutches.

32 | CONFRONTATION
June 30th 2062 · The Talisman

Their names are Joseph and Carson, and they are my beloved sons.

I cannot find them. No matter what I do, I cannot find them. This place is a sprawling one-hundred twelve-thousand square foot complex. Two football fields stacked on top of each other.

It's a massive concrete box with steel-reinforced walls and blast doors. It represents dorms, a massive galley and pantry, communications infrastructure, reserve power containing water and fuel storage, as well as medical facilities, counting dental.

They could be *anywhere* in here.

There are eighteen dormitories and several conference rooms, as well as a massive hall for joint sessions of Congress *and* individual chambers for the Senate and House.

Suddenly, an alarm rings out. It's a klaxon of some kind, reverberating throughout all the halls, deafening at times. We're seven-hundred feet underground, and it echoes throughout the earth all around me. An overhead PA springs to life, and someone calls out.

Intruder alert! Intruder alert! All personnel shelter in place. Run-hide-fight is now in effect. Assailant is on the premises!

Damn. The jig is up! They've found me. Or, at least, they've been alerted to my presence and saw me on camera or something. I don't know.

Where are my sons!? My heart lurches in my throat. I must find them before the guards find me.

Still no sign of them. I'm frantic!

The klaxon continues to sound, and I am nowhere nearer to finding my sons. I occasionally stumble upon fleeing staffers, casting dark, frightened eyes upon me and racing away for their safety. Of course! Why not? I'm, after all, a menace, according to Lynch.

I saw her broadcast as well. I'm 'masquerading as a normal human being.' I'm, 'quite simply, a malevolent presence.' I 'don't have anyone's best interests at heart.' I possess 'unique giftings and can appear to defy logic in my behavior.' I 'can teleport, disappearing and reappearing at will.' I remember all of it. I was just as shocked as any of them to hear her drop my name on the coattails of all of that. I, like Onyx, initially thought she was referring to The Zorander.

I *thought* they were going to help me.

I was wrong.

And now I must make it right.

But these people don't trust me to do so; they regard me with ill will and malice, assuming the worst of me. A few brave guards draw their sidearms and prepare to shoot. I'm out of there before they can nail me.

Come on, come on, I think to myself, searching in desperation, angst welling up within me. Was all of this a ruse? Cardona – and Lynch – have proved treacherous. Was this just a ploy to get me away from them, to stall, to draw me out into the open so that I could be hurt, captured, or killed?

But everything in Andi's eyes and voice said no. I can still see tear-filled eyes pleading with me. She wants her grandsons safe. Why would she send me elsewhere? Why would she trick me? Isn't it in both of their best interests for me to rescue their grandsons?

"Joseph! Carson!"

Why can't I find them? They have to be here somewhere.

Suddenly, a guard appears from around a corner just as I round it; he hurls his baton at me. I dodge and weave, and his swing goes wide.

"Stop!" I cry, holding my hands up. "I don't want to hurt you!" The man just bares his fangs and lunges at me again. He has some skill with his baton, swinging left, right, as I dodge, dematerialize, and appear behind him. He doesn't know where I am. Now, I grab him from the rear and twist his arm behind him. He cries out in pain, dropping his baton. It thuds around noisily on the corridor floor.

Suddenly, there's another one. A second guard appears down the passageway from us, and he's wielding a sidearm. "Freeze!" he shouts, taking aim. We both gaze at him in alarm. "Don't shoot!" his partner calls, holding up his hands.

I don't need this unnecessary delay. I have to find my boys! Anger rises up within me, welling over into rage. "Put the gun down *now*." I order him, sternly, practically hissing it in his direction. He doesn't comply, inching closer.

"I said, put it down!" I command again. "You don't want to do this. I'm not going to hurt you. Either of you! For the last time, put it *down!*"

This second guard must be infused with some kind of bravado or maniacal audacity, because he inches closer and closer, waiting for me to release his partner. He appears to be zeroing in, going for perfect aim, intent on barely missing his partner but mortally wounding me. I can see his actions through his intent.

I wrap my arms suddenly around his partner, and we're gone – just as the other guard's bullets leave a hot stream in their wake, slicing through the air past where we stood, pulverizing the wall behind us.

Ninety-two to go.

One away or one to stay, and balance anew.

The first guard and I reappear back in the dorms, and I release my grasp on him. He's shell-shocked and shivering. He spins around to face me.

"I was never going to hurt you," I whisper, leveraging a posture of readiness should he spring. However, it's a needless concern: he appears anything but ready for that. He's glancing around wondering what the heck happened and why his environment suddenly changed.

"I'm looking for my sons. Joseph and Carter Mayfield. President Cardona had them transferred here for their safety."

"Ye-yes, I know," he says, holding his hands up and eyeing me suspiciously. He backs away. "They're not here, they're, um-"

I try to be patient, but time is running out. "Where. *Where?!*" I yell.

He stutters and flinches. "Uh, I think down past the door. J-just beyond the twenty-five ton door and outside the briefing room, okay?" He's got his hands up in defense and he continues to back away from me, glancing around for some point of egress and escape. "Th-there is a new room down there set apart from the one with all the bunks. They're down there. Down there, okay?"

"Which way? *Tell me!*" I bark.

He flinches again, pointing to the right. "That way, down there, to the east! Gah!" He turns and bolts to the left, west and back up a passageway. I watch him flee for a moment, desperately hoping he's been truthful.

I turn my gaze to the east.

The room is small, but there are comforts distributed throughout. There are two beds in it, and they've been made. Kept neat and clean, practically along military standards, the beds are made and folded to a nicety, the covers overlapping with parallel, dedicated precision. The pillows have been fluffed.

The table in the corner has been cleared, with silverware and utensils arranged as painstakingly as if the residents here were expecting guests. I walk around. There's a strange scent in here, pungent. Ah yes, the smell of teenagers with their pungent odor, all trapped in a small room while they awaited some fate they loathed, desperate to tick off the hours until they could wander freely upon the grass above again. In that sense, it wasn't all too different from my life trapped in Harvill Hall. I remember…

There are small creature comforts in here. An iPhone. An iPad. Some boxed snacks and sodas. A backpack full of books and notepads.

An unshakeable air stalks this room, filling every corner with a tangible sense of familiarity. I don't know this place, but I know the residents. And then, at last, to dispel all doubt and confirm my suspicion, I see it.

A small picture frame on an end table near the window. A simple four-by-six sits inserted inside it. I approach, slowly, squinting at it and hoping with hope – or *against* it? – that I'll recognize the subjects therein.

I reach down and lift it up to my face. There, clear for all to see, and obvious to my watering eyes, are two young souls that I held in my arms when they were just minutes old.

I remember cradling them and rocking them to sleep, singing them lullabies and cooing to them. Changing their diapers. Playing ball outside. Teaching them to ride their bikes. Regaling them with this father's war stories. Chest-thumping and re-enacting scenes from battling gorgons with reverberating bravado.

It's them. They voicelessly stare back at me with former approval, trapped in time. For these are my sons, and their smiles are now unknown to me.   I have not spoken to them in years, as I've tried to respect their wishes.

Next to the picture frame is a note, hastily scrawled in pen and placed in a position of attention, perpendicular and angled in stark contrast to the precision of the rest of the room. My eyes are drawn to it.

Dad,

He has us. The Zorander. He wants the locations of everyone else as well. He'll kill us, dad. He wants you to meet him at noon CEST tomorrow in Svalbard.

I'm sorry, Dad…

The handwriting is hastily written and trails off, but there is no mistaking the penmanship of my firstborn. *Joseph.* Whether or not Carson was in pain when Joseph wrote it, I don't know. A chill runs down my spine. My boys! My sons! Taken by The Zorander! I am too late!

I cannot see anymore. My eyes are wet with tears, overrun by emotion and cloudy now, as I crumple up the note and hold it to my lips in fright. A tremor spills through my chest, and my muscles quake. A slow howl rises within me, seeking exit from my lungs, and I let out a monstrous and unrestrained cry of despondency. The room practically buckles and cracks as I amaze myself with my roar.

With horror, I realize now that the overhead PA announcement wasn't about *me* at all. It was about my greatest nightmare, my largest threat, my chief bane, and the one who has the power to undo all of my progress and set flame to all my yearning.

The Zorander.

He has my sons!

Footsteps. Many of them. Running down the hall toward the room I'm in.

I open my eyes. I see clearly now.

I hear everything.

I swallow with determination as I stare deeply and longingly at the photo, remembering my sons. The glyphs on my suit flash blue, echoing my agony and my budding resolve, aching and growing within me.

I cannot abandon them. What's more, these simple fools won't have me. They burst in, guns blazing, shooting wildly, connecting with nothing but air.

I will save my sons, even if it means losing Janine. They are the last ones I love, and the most precious.

Their names are Joseph and Carson, and they are sons of the Talisman… The Iskander.

TO BE CONTINUED

AFTERWORD

I should have known that it would be inevitable. I really should have known. But I do know it now. I cannot get away from the *Dissonance*verse which I crafted in 2024. It is a super compelling story filled with beloved narratives that are deep-set in my heart, with characters who forever cry out for their respective resurrections in new stories.

I really struggled with the *Talisman* series. One thing that most readers might not know about me is that I reverse-engineer my books. I did the same thing as a musician: I design the end product first, and then I have something visual to look forward to, to focus on, to drum up excitement about. It gives me a target to aim for. If the cover is attractive, I *want* to write a good story to match it. Concordantly, that's exactly what I did with the *Talisman* series. I designed the covers first, got excited about what they could mean, the mystery and allure behind them, the potential story behind that image, and 'where to from here?'

This time, however, the reverse engineering didn't make it any easier. I simply couldn't come up with the story. It took something drastic, and something I never thought I would do. In full disclosure, I actually used Grok to drum up ideas for a story. I did it three times, in fact, and each time, Grok offered me five potential storylines to possibly pursue.

I hated every single one of them. Seriously. They only served to fuel my loathing and disdain for all things AI. We are an Apple family – I also despise the Android ecosystem – but I will *not* use the Artificial Intelligence features on it. AI is foisted upon us at every turn these days, and I'm sick of it. There's a *reason* it's called 'Artificial,' people.

Anyway, back to Grok. After seeing the results that it vomited out, I couldn't wrap my head around two things: 1) the stories actually came from AI. And 2), I just didn't like any of them. They were all rubbish! I thought to myself, *I can come up with something so much better.* So, I did.

But it wasn't until I stumbled upon something that was sitting there, right under my nose the entire time, that my excitement for this story increased exponentially. The answer was always right there in the name; in both the title *and* the subtitle, in fact, so I'm not exactly sure why it escaped me. Nevertheless, it did.

The story was always going to be about a mysterious interloper, a vigilante striving for balance, and trying to regain that which he lost… but it wasn't until I put a name on him – a very, ahem, *familiar* name, both to myself and my readers, that a roaring fire was lit under my bum to get me moving.

That name… was Liam 'Fox' Mayfield. You might know him better as 'Foxy' (so dubbed by Jet Shipley) from the *Dissonance* hexalogy.

I felt Foxy had a great story to tell. I also felt there was a great deal of story to plumb, given where he had come from, and who he subsequently had become. Granted, he recounted his childhood history for Jet in *Dissonance Volume II: Reckoning* while they were at Mammoth Cave. As with many of the personal stories in those novels, his was no less laden with tragedy and grief. But it was the story of what happened following *Dissonance Volume IV: Relentless* that intrigued me as well. Where did the gorgons go? How was the cleanup and restoration of Earth going? What would happen if someone ran into a rogue gorgon? If there is a future story, whose vantage point do I tell it from?

The lot fell to Foxy, and my eyes were opened. From then on, it was smooth sailing. As I said, it was inevitable. His father-in-law, President Vance Cardona, once called him the "best natural fighter I think I've ever seen." Foxy himself proved that he was valiant in the wars of 2042 and 2045. He was always a relatively cheery kid, full of reckless optimism and unflappable spirit. So, I asked myself one question.

What would happen if that optimism and spirit were compromised? That's where this story began. As many of my readers will readily recognize, Jet himself called Foxy his 'talisman' at Wright-Patterson Air Force Base in chapter 3 of *Dissonance Volume III: Renegade.* That chapter is called *Talisman.* And the chapter before that had such a great title as well. *Subterfuge.* So, it was fate, really.

Liam 'Fox' Mayfield is the new star of the show, and I hope my readers will enjoy the tie-in to the original *Dissonance* hexalogy because of it.

Many thanks to my beloved wife Janine for editing my novel with such grace, professionalism and skill. Oh! And for putting up with me eagerly asking "Where are you at?" twenty-seven times in a row. Thank you once again to Jeannine Dryden, Walker Armstrong and Victoria Richmond for being such incredibly awesome ARC readers. And thank you to Victoria, Rhonda Davis and Vance Pease for reviewing my audiobooks for errors and clarity.

As always, thank YOU to all of my beloved readers, who continue to support my authoring journey. There is truly nothing like it, and there is truly nothing like you. Get ready for the sequels, *Talisman: Nexus,* and *Talisman: Halcyon,* coming as soon as I can possibly bring them your way.

Long live The Iskander, Liam 'Foxy' Mayfield.

The Talisman.

With love,

Aaron Ryan

ABOUT THE AUTHOR

Award-winning and bestselling multi-genre Christian author, speaker and voice actor Aaron Ryan lives in Washington with his wife and two sons, along with Macy the dog, Winston & Tibbles the cats, and a finch named Fry.

He is the prolific author of over 50 books, including the bestselling *Dissonance* 6-book alien invasion saga, the dystopian Christian fiction trilogies *Carbon* and *The End*, the *Talisman* epic space opera, the sci-fi thrillers *Forecast, The Slide, Blood Echoes, The Darkness Within* and *The Phoenix Experiment*, the nonfiction books *God Is Not Santa, You are my whole Earth: A Daddy's love for his Sons*, and *You're Going Straight To Helen (In A Handbasket),* business guides, literary criticism, 6 kids picture books and more.

When he was in second grade, he was tasked with writing a creative assignment: a fictional book. And thus, *The Electric Boy* was born: a simple novella full of intrigue, fantasy, and 7-year-old wits that electrified Aaron's desire to write. From that point forward, Aaron evolved into a creative soul that desired to create.

He enjoys the arts, media, music, performing, poetry, and being a daddy. In his lifetime he has been an author, voiceover artist, wedding videographer, stage performer, musician, producer, rock/pop artist, executive assistant, service manager, paperboy, CSR, poet, tech support, worship leader, and more. The diversity of his life experiences gives him a unique approach to business, life, ministry, faith, and entertainment.

Aaron's favorite author by far is J.R.R. Tolkien, but he also enjoys Suzanne Collins, James S.A. Corey, Michael Crichton, Marie Lu, Madeleine L'Engle, John Grisham, Tom Clancy, Tim Lebbon, Christopher Golden, C.S. Lewis, Stephen King and Dave Barry. Aaron has always had a passion for storytelling.

Visit his website at https://www.authoraaronryan.com, join his exclusive Facebook group at https://authoraaronryangroup.com, or check out his store at https://authoraaronryanstore.com.

Reviews

If you liked this or any of my books, please visit the Amazon and Goodreads pages for the specific book(s) and leave a positive review. Once it shows up, email the screenshot to me@authoraaronryan.com please, for a discount on your next book purchase from me! Thank you so much. Reviews really do help a ton, and I'm so very grateful for you taking the time.

Connect with Aaron

Feel free to check out the following links for further information on Aaron:

Subscribe to Aaron's blog for free giveaways, news and new releases at **authoraaronryan.com/blog**

Join the Author Aaron Ryan Facebook community at
facebook.com/groups/authoraaronryan

Subscribe to Aaron's YouTube channel at
youtube.com/@authoraaronryan

Visit Aaron's social media links to connect with him at
dot.cards/authoraaronryan

Visit Aaron's website at **authoraaronryan.com**

Follow Aaron on IMDb at
www.imdb.com/name/nm5976186/

ALSO BY THE AUTHOR

As Aaron Ryan:

1. *Dissonance Volume I: Reality*
2. *Dissonance Volume II: Reckoning*
3. *Dissonance Volume III: Renegade*
4. *Dissonance Volume IV: Relentless*

5. *Dissonance Volume Zero: Revelation*
6. *Dissonance Volume Up: Rising*
7. *The Complete Dissonance Alien Invasion Saga*
8. *The End: Alpha*
9. *The End: Omicron*
10. *The End: Omega*
11. *The Complete "The End" Christian Dystopian Saga*
12. *Carbon Volume I: Programming*
13. *Carbon Volume II: Reformatting*
14. *Carbon Volume III: Rebooting*
15. *The Complete Carbon Trilogy*
16. *Forecast*
17. *The Slide*
18. *The Phoenix Experiment*
19. *Thrillerumvirate*
20. *Blood Echoes*
21. *The Darkness Within*
22. *Talisman: Subterfuge*
23. *Talisman: Nexus*
24. *Talisman: Halcyon*
25. *The Complete Talisman Series*
26. *The Ring of Truth*
27. *The Sword of Joy*
28. *The Book of Power*
29. *The Christian Kids Values, Identity & Affirmation Series*
30. *The Super Ordinary Heroes Series: Empathy*
31. *The Super Ordinary Heroes Series: The Invisibility Cape*
32. *The Super Ordinary Heroes Series: The Time-stopping Hug*
33. *God Is Not Santa*

Gratitude is a hallmark of our home. At my wedding, I was labeled by my cousin as a "rabid over-thanker."

I have no such intention of losing this esteemed reputation.

So with that, once again, THANK YOU – rabidly – *each* and *every* one of you – for reading my books, and for leaving reviews online about them, and for telling your friends and family about them. Really, thank you from the deepest and warmest places in my heart.